CEO'S BABY SCANDAL

AVA GRAY

ALSO BY AVA GRAY

ONTEMPORARY ROMANCE
Mafia Kingpins Series
His to Own
His to Protect
His to Win

The Valkov Bratva Series
Stolen by the Bratva
Kept by the Bratva

Festive Flames Series
Silver Hills' Christmas Miracle

Harem Hearts Series
3 SEAL Daddies for Christmas
Small Town Sparks
Her Protector Daddies

Her Alpha Bosses
The Mafia's Surprise Gift

The Billionaire Mafia Series

Knocked Up by the Mafia
Stolen by the Mafia
Claimed by the Mafia
Arranged by the Mafia
Charmed by the Mafia

Alpha Billionaire Series

Secret Baby with Brother's Best Friend
Just Pretending
Loving The One I Should Hate
Billionaire and the Barista
Coming Home
Doctor Daddy
Baby Surprise
A Fake Fiancée for Christmas
Hot Mess
Love to Hate You - The Beckett Billionaires
Just Another Chance - The Beckett Billionaires
Valentine's Day Proposal
The Wrong Choice - Difficult Choices
The Right Choice - Difficult Choices
SEALed by a Kiss
The Boss's Unexpected Surprise
Twins for the Playboy
When We Meet Again
The Rules We Break
Secret Baby with my Boss's Brother
Frosty Beginnings
Silver Fox Billionaire

Taken by the Major
Daddy's Unexpected Gift
Off Limits
Boss's Baby Surprise

Playing with Trouble Series:
Chasing What's Mine
Claiming What's Mine
Protecting What's Mine
Saving What's Mine

The Beckett Billionaires Series:
Love to Hate You
Just Another Chance

Standalone's:
Ruthless Love
The Best Friend Affair

PARANORMAL ROMANCE

Maple Lake Shifters Series:
Omega Vanished
Omega Exiled
Omega Coveted
Omega Bonded

Everton Falls Mated Love Series:
The Alpha's Mate

The Wolf's Wild Mate
Saving His Mate
Fighting For His Mate

Dragons of Las Vegas Series:
Thin Ice
Silver Lining
A Spark in the Dark
Fire & Ice
Dragons of Las Vegas Boxed Set (The Complete Series)

Standalone's:
Fiery Kiss
Wild Fate

BLURB

"You're pregnant with my twins?! Why didn't you tell me sooner?"

How did I end up here?

1. Trapped in my **CEO's office**
2. His kisses still *burning* on my lips
3. **Two secrets** growing inside me
4. And both our families ready for *war*

One forbidden office romance.
   Two heartbeats I can't explain.
   Three months to hide the truth.
   Zero ways this ends well.

I'm the **king** of the boardroom.
   She's the assistant who brought me to my *knees*.
   One taste of her sweetness,
   And I *broke* all my rules.

They say she's *beneath* me.

Too young. Too innocent. Too poor.
But they don't know what I know—
She's carrying my empire's **future**.

One taste of *forbidden* fruit,
    Two beating hearts beneath her own,
    And a love that *defies* all rules.
    This scandal just became my greatest **victory**.

But someone wants to **destroy** us—
    And they're closing in *fast*.
    The question isn't *if* we'll fall...
    It's **who's pulling the strings**.

Author's Note: CEO's Baby Scandal is a steamy, forbidden office romance featuring an age-gap relationship, surprise twins, and a HEA. Contains mature themes and scenes that will make your kindle melt.

1

EMILY

I knew taking the job as an assistant at a law firm wasn't the best use of my degree in business management, but the pay was decent and I hadn't gotten any other call backs. I stood near reception of the prestigious firm and waited for my boss to greet me. The interview had gone well. She liked my resume and the fact that I could type more than fifty words per minute. So, here I was, ready for my first day.

Olivia strolled out of the office with a file in hand, staring down at it. She wore a Casper suit, red with a cream silk blouse beneath it. It put to shame my black slacks and white button-down, but I hadn't had time or money to go shopping for a new wardrobe. I knew everyone in this place would be better dressed than I was the second I saw the receptionist with her Prada bag.

"Ms. Carter, it's so good to see you again." I offered my hand, but when her eyes popped up from the file in her hand, she barely acknowledged my presence. I stood patiently, retracting my offered handshake, and clutched my purse in front of myself. My friendly, down-home personality might not fit in among powerful attorneys, but that didn't mean I wasn't going to be polite.

"Follow me," she said dryly. Without looking up, she turned and headed back into the office. I glanced at the receptionist who was busy typing at her computer and smacking her gum.

It was an odd greeting for the first day of work, but I hadn't known what to expect. Life in Monroe County was much different from here in Chicago. Everyone knew everyone, and that was why I left. Well, one of the reasons. I had many—including overprotective parents and a thirst to see the world. Chicago meant a fresh start and the beginning of a great adventure. Besides, my best friend, Charlotte, lived here, which made it all the more appealing.

We walked past offices with plaques on the doors indicating whose office they were. Most of them had windows, but the blinds were shut. When we got to Olivia's office, she pushed the door open, the file in her hand finally tucked under her arm. She waltzed in and dropped the file on her desk. A small desk sat outside the door with a cup of pencils and a phone. I glanced at it as I followed her in.

"So, you're four minutes late on the first day. Not a great impression. I'll overlook that because traffic is a bitch in this city at this time of day. Don't let it happen again." She had her blonde hair pulled back tightly into a bun which made her eyes draw out into thin slits, making her look of Asian descent.

"Of course, my apologies. I've only lived in Chicago for a few months. I'm still learning the ropes."

"Good, well, enough with pleasantries. Today will be about meeting everyone, learning their roles, and your position in helping them. I want to take you to meet the directors and officers, but first you need to understand that I am your boss. You'll assist me, mainly, though there will be days when you are needed elsewhere." She tapped her long, manicured fingers on the corner of her desk and stared at me as if she needed a response. I had no clue what to say to her.

"Yes, ma'am."

"Well, follow me." She charged out the door into the hall again and tapped the desk. "Purse here."

Her gait was so quick, I had to scurry to keep up after stuffing my purse into the top drawer of the desk. I straightened my top and raced after her. "This is Tony's office, and Grace is here." She pointed at doors that were clearly labeled as if I couldn't read. I wasn't offended by that. I had no time to be. She opened the door at the end of the hall and stood in it. "This is the conference room. Get used to delivering coffee here."

I nodded. I knew I was just an assistant, and I figured my role wouldn't be glamorous, but I'd hoped for more than coffee duty and making copies of files. She breezed past me and back up the hallway, so I scurried along, making a mental note of each office door and whose name was on it. Most had no title along with the name, but a few did. Grace was a junior partner—good to know. Tony had no label. Michael Blake and Benjamin Jameson both had "Sr. Partner" emblazoned on their placards. I had a lot of names to memorize.

Olivia led me past reception and down a shorter hallway the opposite direction. We passed another room that had a large table, perhaps a board room. Then we approached an office with a bright gold plaque on it.

"Here is the office of our head partner and CEO of the firm, Daniel Jacobs." She knocked quietly and waited. "Mr. Jacobs doesn't like to be disturbed, so never enter his office without being requested. Also, be very direct with him, no games or being vague. You'll likely end up helping each of the partners at some point, but as the head of the company, Jacobs comes first. Anything he asks, you do it. Got it?"

I opened my mouth to answer as I heard a voice call from the other side of the door. Her pep talk was intimidating. Everyone in Chicago knew the name of the firm, and Jacobs's face was plastered on billboards and city buses. I thought I'd be working with paralegals and secretaries. I had no clue I would be required to assist the partners, which made my stomach flip-flop when I followed her into the room and saw the man himself seated behind his desk.

"Sir, this is..." She turned and snapped her fingers as if having forgotten my name, so I supplied it for her.

"Emily Kline, sir." I stepped forward and thrust my hand out again, only this time, it was received. "Nice to meet you."

His hand was soft but strong. Olivia continued introducing me based on my accolades, which weren't many, but Mr. Jacobs never broke eye contact. There was a mischievousness there in his gaze that sparked my interest. He was striking, dark hair, dark eyes. For a man almost fifteen years older than me I found him very attractive. I wasn't sure if it was I who was still holding his hand, or if he just hadn't let go yet.

"So, for now, she will work solely with me, but I will make her available to you whenever you need copies made or if Jill is out." Olivia's introduction concluded, and I stepped back. My fingers tingled where he'd touched them. He gawked at me for a moment like I was a piece of meat, but a guy that hot... I didn't mind.

"Welcome to Jacobs, Blake, Jameson and Gonzalez, Ms. Kline." Mr. Jacobs stood, pushing his chair away. "I hope Olivia has treated you kindly."

I felt acutely aware that the top button of my blouse was open. I had debated whether to button it or leave it open before leaving the house. In Monroe County, I'd have been the talk of the town. Mrs. Grubel would have called me the town slut for sure, but here in the city, I noticed most women weren't afraid to show a little cleavage. Olivia paid no attention to it, and I could see why. Half of her chest was exposed beneath her silk blouse.

"Yes, she's been very kind." I lied. She hadn't been kind, nor unkind, just curt. I clasped my hands in front of myself and swallowed hard. He was definitely looking at my breasts. My cheeks burned because I liked the idea that he was attracted to me.

"Well, if you don't have anything for me, I'll show Emily the rest of the office." Olivia crossed her arms over her chest and tapped her foot.

"I'd like to ask her a few questions, Olivia. You are excused."

Her eyes flicked from Mr. Jacobs to me, and she pursed her lips, but she did as she was told and left, closing the door behind her.

If my nerves had been heightened just meeting the man, they were frazzled standing here alone with him. His crystal blue eyes had a dark ring of cerulean around them, and they locked on me again. My chest fluttered. No man this gorgeous had ever taken notice of me, and the fact that he wasn't just a powerful attorney, but my boss's boss, made my insides melt.

"Sir?"

"Sit."

I swallowed hard and obeyed, grateful I had worn sensible shoes and not three-inch stilettos like Olivia. I'd have fallen on my face and made a fool of myself and this man would never look at me twice. I wasn't sure whether I should be flattered by the way he drank me in or intimidated by it. I had no intention of staying an assistant anywhere for very long. My degree should have communicated that to anyone who looked at my resume.

Mr. Jacobs sat and smoothed his tie. "Emily—may I call you that?"

"Yes, please." I nodded, biting my tongue. I sounded like an idiot.

"Emily, I looked over your resume." My chest tightened as he spoke. "It says you have a master's degree in business management from UC Berkeley. You did that all during the pandemic? Incredible. Why do you want to be a mere assistant?" He leaned back in his seat and studied me while I collected my thoughts.

"Well, sir, I don't. I might not be able to use my education here, but I am not planning to be an assistant for life. I moved to Chicago where there are more opportunities, and I accepted this position because it pays well. I will be able to support myself. But it is just a stepping stone to my future. I want a career, not a job."

He nodded appreciatively, and the gleam in his eye only brightened. "Such a wise plan…" His eyes grazed over my chest again, and I looked away nervously, not stopping the grin that spread across my face. "I think it's fantastic that you know where you're going and you're making strides to get there." He stood again, this time reaching out his hand to me. I rose with him and took his hand, which this time was much gentler.

"Emily, if you need anything" —he leaned closer, and his voice thickened into a sultry tone— "and I mean anything, you come to me. I'll make it happen."

I bit my lip and batted my eyelashes. Right now, I needed him to let go of my hand because I was feeling things no assistant should ever feel about their boss, and I could see the hunger in his eyes.

"Uh, thank you, Mr. Jacobs."

"You should call me Daniel." My fingers tingled again as he drew my hand to his lips and kissed them. "It's what my friends call me."

My heart almost stopped. I thought I'd cream my panties right there. My conscience told me that a boss shouldn't act this way toward an employee, but damn if the attention wasn't nice. My sister Evelyn got every boy who ever crossed paths with her. I, however, had been the homely daughter—never dated, never had a boy ask me to a dance. The one time I had a fling was at a college party when Evelyn forced me to go with her, and I had a one-night stand with a frat boy which I later regretted miserably. So this man, with his suave, wavy hair and eyes that bored into my soul... well, he could be obsessed with me if he wanted.

I liked it.

2

DANIEL

I t took exactly twenty seconds for my cock to begin swelling when Olivia brought the new assistant into my office. She had an innocence about her I found intriguing, and her resume boasted some credentials a lot of women her age didn't have. I'd already had a chance to review her qualifications and her headshot and thought she was stunning, but when she walked in I was smitten. She didn't seem to mind my wandering eye, either.

She'd been with us four days now, but I hadn't seen her for more than five minutes. Olivia kept her busy, and I was swamped with work. So, it was a pleasant surprise when Olivia sent her to my office to deliver the briefings I needed for the partner meeting later this afternoon. She was timid, knocking so quietly I almost missed it. And when I beckoned her in, she hovered near the door.

"Mr. Jacobs, I brought the files from Ms. Carter."

"Please, I told you to call me Daniel." I rose, waving my hand at her to come in. She left the door open, much to my disdain, but it was probably better that way. She was intoxicating, and I would be tempted to say untoward things.

"Sorry, uh, Daniel. I have the briefings Ms. Carter sent for you." She handed them to me and took a step back, picking at her fingernails. I knew I was an intimidating man. Everyone cowered in my shadow despite my open personality. I thumbed through them to make sure they were all in order and nodded approvingly.

"Yes, this will do. Thank you, Emily." She smiled softly, and I saw a blush form on her cheeks. "We have an important meeting for the partners, and I've ordered some catering to make sure they all eat well. I need someone to run down to pick it up. I will give you the company credit card. You can take my car. My driver's name is Paul. He'll get you where you need to go, so no worries about directions and such. Think you can handle that?"

She looked confused and glanced at the door, outside of which Jill sat, typing at her computer. "What about your secretary?" Her innocence was truly refreshing. Olivia and Grace would never have questioned me. Jill never spoke out of turn, and here was this blonde beauty, rising to the challenge. I grinned at how bold she was.

"Jill has a daughter on the school swim team and they have a meet this afternoon, so she can't pick it up for me. That leaves you. Unless you have other plans."

Her head snapped around to see me, and she shook it. "No, sir. No other plans. I'm at your service."

"Good. Then, I'll shoot you an email with the details." I reached into my pocket and pulled out my company credit card. It was a good test of her integrity. The card had no limit, and I hadn't so much as offered it to Olivia, let alone an assistant. "Here." I offered her the card, and she hesitated to take it, but I insisted. "You'll have to pay for it. Keep a receipt for Barbra. She'll nag me about expenditures if I don't give her one. And—"

"Got it." She grinned and winked at me. "My mom was the same way. I'll take good care of you."

She had no idea what that wink and grin did to me, or probably how gorgeous she was at all. She was modest, and I liked it. "Thank you." I sat back down and started into the files, and she turned to walk away, and I looked up and watched her ass sway with each step. She wore a pencil skirt today, a bit fancier than the slacks I'd seen her in earlier this week. The dark material hugged her thighs and showed off her muscular calves.

"Oh, and Emily?" I called after her, wanting nothing more than to see her striking smile again.

"Yes, sir?"

"When you get here with the food, just bring it straight to us in the conference room. No need to knock."

There it was, the smile of the century. "Of course, sir."

"Daniel," I corrected.

"Daniel," she said, blushing.

My dick was out of control. When I sat down, it was because I felt myself swelling again, because I normally stood as a matter of principle. When a lady was standing, the men in the room should be also. It was a respect thing. But damn, my body betrayed me. I knew I had to get this under control. I didn't want Emily to think I was flirting with her as her boss, but just as a man who found her highly attractive.

I tried to focus on work all day, but it was a struggle. As I sat in the conference room across from Michael and Grace, anticipation rose in my gut. We were just chatting, waiting on our late lunch to be delivered by Emily and for Ben to show up, but I was as tense as if I were in a power meeting with one of our larger clients. The way she kept me waiting was torture.

A knock came at the door and Emily entered. I rose immediately and waved her over. "Come in, come in. I told you, you didn't have to knock."

She blushed and juggled the bags of takeout. "Sorry, they were running a little behind. Paul got stuck in traffic. It was horrible." She set the bags down and began opening them. Her fingers fumbled nervously, and I couldn't decide if it was because she walked in on the meeting of all the partners or if she felt flustered.

"Here, let me help you." Grace pulled one of the bags toward herself and tore it open, and Emily's cheeks turned pink.

She backed away as Grace set the food out, and I struck up a conversation to keep her in the room a bit longer. "Emily, how has your first week been so far? Is Olivia keeping you busy?" I never paid attention to other staff members. I usually left that to our paralegals or HR. Michael gave me an odd expression, but I ignored him.

"So far, so good. I've just been doing some filing, mostly, coffee runs, and I got Michael's dry cleaning for him yesterday." Her eyes flicked nervously at my partner and then back to her hands.

"Excellent, well I hope you're settling in well."

She turned her gaze up to meet mine, and I couldn't help but notice how her eyes sparkled. Beauty didn't begin to describe her. She was elegance and class mixed with a down home charm any man would love. I stared at her a bit too long, noticing the way one cheek had a dimple while the other didn't.

"That will be all, Ms. Kline." Michael dismissed her, and she bowed at the shoulder before excusing herself.

I watched again as she walked toward the door, hips swaying with each step. It was like she purposely tried to catch my attention, each step taunting me to keep my gaze fixed on her perky ass. She glanced over her shoulder as she reached the door and caught my eye. I could have sworn she winked at me. And long after she had gone, I remained staring at the door, despite having sat down to enjoy my meal.

"You seem to be taken with the new assistant." Michael's comment came as being a bit forward to me. We typically stayed out of each other's personal lives. I hadn't commented on his relationships—not even when he had been divorced by his wife for cheating on her with a lawyer at the district attorney's office.

"Yes, well she's quite stunning. Don't you think?" I peeled the plastic lid off my roast turkey and vegetables and picked up my fork.

Grace shook her head, her eyebrows rising as she did. She was the mother hen around the place, always making sure staff and partners alike toed the line. She chewed her food in silence, though I had a sinking suspicion that had she not had a mouth full of food at the time, she'd have commented too.

"She's an employee, Daniel. It's bad news." Michael cracked open a soda he pulled from one of the brown paper bags and sipped it. "It's a lawsuit waiting to happen. Women don't mess around anymore."

I scoffed as I took a bite of turkey. The flavors melted on my tongue, almost as deliciously as I was certain Emily would if I could just taste her. Michael had a point. The world went crazy over the last "me too" movement, and the climate in the workplace changed dramatically. I'd had to bring in an expert for sensitivity training to ensure everyone knew what constituted as sexual harassment. But this wasn't that. I would never impose my authority on any employee in that way. If Emily didn't like my advances, I'd control myself.

But the look she'd given me when she walked out the door just then hadn't been a look of intimidation. She liked how I paid extra attention to her. After I swallowed my bite of food, I said, "Well I don't think you have to worry about that because I know how to control myself."

"It's just bad optics, Dan." Grace had gotten into an uncomfortable habit of calling me by the nickname, and it bothered me. "Imagine the media gets wind of the CEO dating his assistant. She's not even your assistant, either. She's Olivia's. Even if she didn't cry wolf, the press would insinuate it. Or worse, destroy the girl's reputation by throwing her under the bus as the tramp who is sleeping her way to the top."

"No reputable media would do that." I wiped my mouth and continued. "They'd have to have some reason to come after me, anyway. I keep my nose clean. The tabloids can take a hike. Everyone knows they only print useless drivel, and if they printed a story like that, I'd just sue for libel."

The door opened and Ben walked in, followed by Olivia. They were engaged in a conversation about their weekend plans, and I was glad for the distraction. I did care what my partners thought about who I dated. Emily was the first woman who crossed my path who ticked off all the boxes on my list—smart, driven, gorgeous, available, and best of all, humble. I'd be a fool if I didn't at least get to know her better.

"Ah, you got lunch. Great, I'm starving." Ben sat down across from me and pulled a dish of food toward himself. I took the opportunity to change the subject and get the meeting rolling.

"Olivia, once we're done eating, I'll have you start the discussion by going over the briefs you sent to me earlier. We have our work cut out for us on this one." I took another bite of turkey, and Olivia started in with her opinions on the big business case we were working on, but my mind was only on one thing.

Emily Kline was a rare jewel who entered my life at a time when I had just enough free time to entertain the idea of testing the waters with her. Things at the firm were going well, as was life outside the firm. If she was half as perfect as I believed her to be, I wanted her to be a fixture in my life. I hadn't seen a ring on her finger, though she could be dating someone. Still, I was going by the wise words my college basketball coach told me. "Dating ain't married." It was his awkward way of saying if someone isn't married, they're still available.

That put Emily squarely on my radar. And I never missed my target.

3

EMILY

I juggled the two bags of takeout in my hands. For the second day in a row, Mr. Jacobs had ordered food to be brought in. At least this time I wasn't asked to go out and get it. The DoorDash driver brought it right to the building, though he refused to bring it up to the offices. So, I'd taken the elevator down to get it and rode back up to our floor with the scent of Mexican food filling my nostrils. My stomach growled the entire way. I still had forty minutes until I could take lunch, and I was starving.

With my hands full, it was difficult to knock on Daniel's office door, so I was glad to see it had been left ajar. As I approached, I could see him leaned back in his chair speaking to someone on the phone. I lingered there, not eavesdropping, as he finished, and when he hung up, I gently pushed the door open.

"Sorry, Mr. Jacobs, the door was open. I have your lunch." I felt awkward just walking in, especially after Olivia had told me not to ever enter his office without being invited. He looked up at me and waved me over as he typed something on his computer. It looked like he was focusing, so I set the bags on the corner of his desk and hurried back toward the door, not wanting to disrupt him. I had my hand on the doorknob when he called out to me.

"Emily, please stay."

I froze in place, feeling like I had done something wrong. It was only my fifth day on the job, and I just wanted to do a good job for everyone, but I had made a horrible mistake by not knocking.

"And close the door, please."

I swallowed a lump in my throat as I shut the door quietly and turned to face him. The rebuke was warranted. I knew I hadn't followed instructions, but my hands were full and the door was open, so I hadn't thought it would be a big deal to slip in, set the food down, and slip out. I stayed by the door as he finished whatever it was he was doing and braced myself for an angry eruption, or at the very least, a lecture.

He moved some files off his desk and pulled the bags of food toward himself. "Come sit," he ordered as he opened the first bag.

Confused, I hesitantly strolled to the chairs situated across from his desk and sat down. He unpacked the dishes, foil tins with paper lids on them. Steam rose from the aromatic food as he uncovered the tins and made my mouth water.

"Uh, sir…"

"Shh," he interrupted. "Just getting lunch ready."

My stomach growled loudly. I had a few things to get done before I could leave and get my own lunch, and the longer I sat watching him unveil this veritable feast in front of me, torturing my tastebuds, the less time I'd have to finish those tasks and get my own food. I didn't want to seem impatient, however, and Olivia told me how stern Mr. Jacobs was, so I folded my hands in my lap and tried not to be bothered by the delicious scents wafting my way.

"Chorizo or chicken?" he asked, looking up at me.

"Uh, I'm not sure I know what you're asking."

"I ordered enough for two. Would you like chorizo or chicken?" He tilted the dishes toward me so I could see how delectable they looked. I could tell straight away which one was chicken, slathered in queso and pico, a dollop of sour cream and guacamole topping the salad next to the meat.

"I'm confused." I wondered if this was normal, for the head partner and CEO of the firm to entertain new employees, or if perhaps I was getting special treatment. I'd seen the way he looked at me, and I wasn't shy about returning the not so subtle gazes of attraction.

"I am inviting you to eat with me. If you don't want Mexican, we can go out and get whatever you want."

I was flattered. "Uh, no, sir. I love Mexican food. I think the chicken looks good."

"Here," he said, pushing the tin in my direction. He slid a cutlery pack across the table toward me and pulled the chorizo dish back to his side of the desk. "I'm glad you like it because Mexican is my favorite. I eat it a couple times a week."

Reaching for the plasticware, I couldn't help but look back at the door and wonder if one of the partners or staff members would walk in and interrupt us. They'd see me dining with him and wonder what was going on. I didn't want to be painted as the woman who paid extra attention to the boss in order to get special treatment. Nor did I want to brush off the advances of a very handsome man whom I took a real interest in. The confusion made my appetite wane slightly.

"Don't worry. No one enters this office without being invited."

"Except me," I grumbled, thinking I'd said it quietly enough that he couldn't hear me, but he chuckled.

"True." He unwrapped his cutlery and continued, "But I knew you were coming and I left the door ajar on purpose."

His good humor put me at ease. "Why are you like that?" It was an honest question. I had bosses before who were too strict, guys who liked to hold their power over others to keep them in line. Mr. Jacobs didn't seem that way. At least not to me.

"We handle a lot of very confidential and sensitive information. No one enters my office at any time without being invited because at any given time, I could be on a call or have private documents out."

"So you left the door open for me knowing you wouldn't be handling confidential information?" I peeled the wrapper off the cutlery and unrolled it. I could almost taste the food already.

"Something like that." He winked at me as he took a bite. I was beginning to sense, based on his body language and how friendly he was, that this was more of a social lunch than a business lunch. I didn't mind. He was very handsome and was the first man who'd looked my way since getting to the city.

"Uh, well you know my lunch isn't for about forty minutes." I plunged the fork into the salad and scooped up some sour cream too.

"Your lunch is when the boss says your lunch is. Let me deal with Olivia." After he took a bite, he wiped his mouth then reached beneath his desk and produced two bottles of water. "Here, I almost forgot drinks."

"Oh, thank you." Everything about this lunch felt awkward but somehow right. Like we were on a first date just getting to know each other, not across from his desk during work hours.

"Has anyone ever told you how beautiful you are?" He put his fork down as he opened his bottle of water, and I felt my cheeks burning.

"No, honestly."

"Well, you are. And I want to get to know you better—as a person, not as your boss." His eyes twinkled with mischief. "So, tell me, why UC Berkeley, and why Chicago?"

"Well, I did online school during the pandemic, and UC offered the entire course online. And Chicago always seemed like the place to be. Growing up, I hated being a country girl. I like the hustle and bustle of the city." I ate a bite of the chicken and groaned at how delicious it was. "So good."

"I know, right!" He snickered and continued his friendly interrogation. "You miss your family?"

"Just have my parents and one sister, who lives in Chicago too. And I sort of miss home, but not the way small town life goes. You know?" I liked that he was interested in me as a person. It made me more comfortable with having lunch with him, like he wasn't just after sex the way Mom and Evelyn warned me men were.

"Ah, yes. I grew up in Springfield. Not necessarily a major city, but not a small town. I prefer Chicago too..." He took another bite and chewed, and I took the opportunity to ask a question.

"You have any siblings?"

"One brother." He coughed, choking on his bite of food. "Sorry..."

He sipped his water. "It's just me and my brother, but he's married, so I have a sister-in-law."

"That's nice. My sister is married, but I don't know much about her husband." The conversation lulled for a moment as we ate. The food was so good, and I was grateful that he had invited me.

"What about hobbies? Do you do sports? Art?"

Mr. Jacobs truly seemed interested in me, and I liked that we had some things in common. Growing up with only one sibling, I had at times wished we'd had a bigger family and at other times wished I were an only child. I wondered if he also encountered that. "Uh, yes. I played basketball in high school and ran track. I love reading."

"Wow, me too." He nodded appreciatively as he took another bite then chased it with a drink again. "I was the point guard."

"Small forward." I shrugged and grinned.

"I'll have to take you out for some one-on-one." He leaned over his dish and had another large bite. I was starting to feel really comfortable with him. He ate like any other man, huge bites, messy lips. At least he had the decency to not talk with his mouth full, but he was no different from any other guy I'd met. Not intimidating at all.

"So, you like reading too?" I sipped my water and waited as he finished his bite before answering.

"Yes, I actually love classics. Dostoyevsky is my favorite, but I also like Dumas, Lewis, and I've dabbled in some Dickens."

The list of authors he liked made my heart swoon. We had so many things in common. "Have you read *The Count of Monte Cristo*?" I didn't want to take another bite and break up the flow of the conversation. My mind was hungrier to learn more about him than my stomach was for food.

"I have. One of my favorites, actually. I love how complex the subplots are." I couldn't get over his smile and the way his eyes lit up. "I can't believe how much we have in common. You know, I'm really glad I invited you to have lunch with me. We need to do this more often."

"Yeah, I think so too." If the man hadn't been as attractive to me as he was, this would have sealed the deal. He was cultured but down to earth, honest and bold, and he was interested in me. "If you don't mind my saying so, sir, I think you are probably the most attractive man I've ever met."

He laughed so loud, I thought the entire floor would hear him. When he calmed down, he said, "I think you're pretty gorgeous too, and I think we will be spending a lot more time together in the future, you know, see how well we fit, if we connect…" He offered a seductive look over the fork poised to enter his mouth.

The sudden rush of arousal flooding my groin sent another burst of warmth to my cheeks. "I definitely want to know if we fit together." I wasn't sure if he meant the comment as a double entendre, but I certainly did. And I was positive that I wanted him to fit.

4

DANIEL

The window separating the conference room and the hallway was heavily frosted along the horizon, but I could see the feet of passing staff members all day. The meetings were grueling and I was distracted every time Emily strolled past in her bright pink heels. Just thinking of her made it impossible to focus on work. I wasn't even needed in the meeting, but our client, one of the wealthier investment firms in town, expected my presence. It allowed me to fantasize all day about her.

As the meeting drew to a close, I found myself wondering if she was out to lunch already or if I could invite her to join me again. It would be late lunch, which meant it was likely she had already eaten and I'd be rebuffed, but perhaps I could find another excuse to spend time with her. I shook hands with the clients and excused myself only to find Emily had gone out for lunch with Jill. It was a disappointment, but nothing I wasn't prepared for.

I headed down the elevator to the small coffee shop across from the building. Michael frequented the place because they had amazing sandwiches, so I guessed he'd be there sooner or later. I found a spot in a corner booth and waited, ordering a grilled cheese and French fries. The spot had a perfect view of the office entrance, so I was poised to watch Emily return from her lunch.

She had gotten under my skin in a good way, but so deeply I couldn't shake it. I tried to think about the advice Grace and Michael had given me last week about keeping my distance from her, but a woman that perfect—or seemingly perfect—was a diamond in the rough. I'd dated so many women who had zero in common with me. I didn't want a relationship where I was off doing my thing, and she was off spending my money. I wanted a partnership with someone on the same level as me.

Emily and I had a lot in common. I could see us being very happy reading books and sharing about the complexities of the plots or playing basketball at the local sports club. I could also see us having crazy sex, because God knows my sex drive hadn't slowed down at all in all these years. I needed some young spitfire to keep up with me, not a middle-aged woman who wanted nothing to do with it. And there were a number of other things we had in common.

I didn't see her as a problem, more like the situation was a challenge we had to overcome—if she wanted to date me as much as I wanted to date her.

Before my food was delivered, Michael walked in and spotted me. He placed his own order and made his way across the small dining room to sit across from me.

"Wow, that guy is intense, huh? I can't believe he thinks he doesn't need legal counsel for his business. I'm glad Grace is really good at schmoozing people."

"Look, I've had enough work talk for one day. Let's just enjoy lunch and deal with that when we head back in." I nodded at the waitress as she slid my tray in front of me and collected the number placard indicating which order was mine. The sandwich looked delicious. "Thank you."

She nodded and walked away, and I reached for the bottle of ketchup and slathered my fries in it. "So, there is something I wanted to talk to you about."

"Oh, yeah?" Michael asked. He stole a fry off my tray and popped it in his mouth, speaking with his mouth full. "What's that?"

"Well, you've known me pretty much for two decades." I ate a fry and collected my thoughts before continuing. "You know I'm a very picky man with high standards."

He chuckled and stole another fry. Before putting it in his mouth, he said, "That's the understatement of the century. You've had what, two serious relationships?"

"Three, but I'm not counting." I rolled my eyes at his stupid grin. "My point is, it takes a very special person to cross my radar and convince me they're worth taking a shot on. Sure, I've dated plenty of women, but I haven't met more than four worth taking on a second date, and that says something." The waitress returned bringing Michael's lunch. He dismissed her with a wave of the hand and hoisted his massive chicken wrap to his mouth and took a large bite.

Again speaking with his mouth full, he said, "So, who's lucky number four?" It was disgusting watching bits of food dribble from his mouth to his tray, but that was Michael. A total slob.

"That new assistant, Emily, is right up my alley, man, and it's not because she's gorgeous. We have a lot in common. She's easy to talk to. We had lunch a few times over the past week or so since she started, and I like her personality. She has a good head on her shoulders."

The minute I told him who had piqued my interest, he scowled, but I kept talking. He wouldn't cut me off, and it gave him time to swallow his food so I didn't wear his lunch on my suit coat. I knew he had an opinion about it because he'd already given it to me last week, but at that point, I hadn't even had a chance to sit and talk with her yet. Now that I had, things were different. It wasn't just sexual attraction—though I definitely found her arousing.

Instead of lecturing me like I expected him to, Michael took another bite of food. It gave me an opportunity to expound on why this was such a dilemma for me, though maybe I was overthinking things.

"I get that it could be portrayed as wrong for me to pursue her because she is an employee, but I think I could manage to keep the job separated from the personal side. Do you think it's wrong to ask her out? And how do I make it clear to her that it will in no way increase her chances of moving up within the company if she dates me? Not only that, but how can I ensure that she isn't responding to me based on some sort of feeling of pressure that she has to or she'll lose her job?" I shook my head and took a bite of my grilled cheese.

The thoughts kept running through my head that if I had met her on the street or at a bar, we wouldn't be having this conversation. Emily was much younger than me, twelve years, to be exact, but that wasn't a hindrance in my mind. Once you hit twenty-one, age was just a number. It was the job that complicated things.

"I tried to tell you the other day. It's a bad idea. You're looking at bad press, complications within the office like drama and such. And what if she does just feel pressured to date you because you are her boss and she doesn't want to turn you down for fear of being fired? Those are all really valid things. It's just a disaster waiting to happen, Dan."

I chewed while I listened to him, but I couldn't get the thought out of my mind that it didn't have to be that way. We were grown adults. If she didn't want to date me, I'd find some other woman somewhere and put my mind at ease—at least, I tried to convince myself I would do that. Chances were that if she rejected me, I'd probably go home and lick my wounds and sulk.

"Yeah, but—"

"Listen," Michael said, cutting me off, "I get that she seems so special, but there are a million other women out there who could take her place easily. I say, if you think it's a real chance, have Olivia cut her loose now. That way, you're free to date her."

"That's insane. She hasn't done anything to warrant a termination. I could disrupt her finances. She could end up homeless or something, just so I can date her?" It was absurd that Michael thought that was a good idea.

"Well then, shut it down. It's too risky, and you know it. You can't afford a scandal in your life, not to mention what your parents would think. She's practically a child still. You don't need that hassle. Whatever happened to Keri?"

Just the name of my ex was enough to get me hot beneath the collar. I lost my appetite and pushed my plate away. "Keri is history, Mike. You know that. It was a set up from the beginning, and I only dated her to humor my parents."

"Just saying." He continued to eat as if he were ravenous, but I was finished.

"I think I'm going to head back. I want to catch Em before she heads up." I collected my tray and scooted out of the booth.

"You're already using nicknames?" Michael scoffed and shook his head at me again. It seemed his eyes liked to roll around in his head a lot lately. "Cut it off, Daniel. It's bad news. I'm telling you, it's going to go sideways real fast, and you're going to wish you had listened to me."

"Thank you for your advice, Michael, but as my oldest and truest friend, you know I'm not going to listen to it." I chuckled and expected him to catch the joke, but his glower stayed firmly intact.

"I'll see you back at the office." I strolled away, dumping my tray off at the busing station before leaving the shop. I had never been one to take the safe route. If I had, I wouldn't be head partner in the highest-grossing firm in the state. Sometimes risks paid off, and this was a gamble I was willing to bet on.

5

EMILY

I knocked on Daniel's office door and waited. It was just after seven, and he'd only been in for around twenty minutes. He, Olivia, and I were the only ones in this early. I wanted to get a jump on filing, but as soon as I walked in, Olivia told me Jill was out today and I had to be Mr. Jacobs's "little helper" today. I hated the term and felt it was a demeaning way to treat someone of my age, but I didn't complain. Olivia had a few rough edges, but she was a good boss.

"Come in," he called, so I pushed the door open and let myself in. His back was to the door as I entered. He was sorting through a filing cabinet that sat behind his desk. "Just leave it on the desk." He had to be expecting his coffee. I wondered if it was a regular thing Jill did for him.

I traipsed across the large room, having shut the door behind me. My heel caught on the deep pile of the throw rug, and I stumbled, sloshing coffee out of the cup onto the floor. "Oh, God!" The coffee burned my hand, but I was more concerned about the puddle I left on the floor. Mr. Jacobs turned around and looked up at me with a surprised look. "Gosh, I'm sorry." I hurried to the desk and set the cup down, grabbing a few tissues from the box on his desk. "I'll clean it up."

"Emily, I wasn't expecting you. Where's Jill?" He rose and buttoned his jacket as he stood there watching me fumble with the tissues.

"Uh, Jill called in sick, so Olivia said I'm yours for the day." I shrugged and turned back to the mess. It would take several tissues to clean the puddle off the floor, and the carpet would likely be stained. I was on all fours, pressing the tissues into the soggy area rug when I heard Daniel whistle a long, drawn out shrill.

I stopped and looked back over my shoulder at him. He was staring at my ass with eyes wide open, practically drooling.

"You're, uh... I'm." He stumbled with his words, and I snickered. He was blushing, and I was feeling a bit saucy this morning.

"You like the view or something?" I knew it was wrong to flirt with him, but I couldn't help myself. We'd had lunch several times, always skirting the obvious sexual tension between us. He'd made comments about seeing if we "fit" together, which I had played along with.

I kept soaking the mess up with tissues and let him enjoy looking at me. I didn't see the harm in his enjoying the way my body looked. We had already discussed getting to know each other better, and with the things I'd learned so far, I knew I really liked him. So when I stood to retrieve more tissues, I made sure to really give him something to gawk at. I stood slowly, rising to my feet and ensuring I remained bent over right in front of him for a few seconds.

"Now you're just teasing me."

I grinned at his comment, but my back was to him, so I forced my face into a placid expression and turned around to toss the soiled tissues in the trash before reaching for more. "I'm not teasing. I'm just cleaning up a mess I made." I shrugged and plucked a few more tissues from the box. "I don't tease." I winked at him and headed back for the mess, offering him the same view as when I rose.

"God, woman, you're driving me mad. If you aren't teasing me, then either follow through or—"

"Or leave you alone?" I asked cheekily. This time, I didn't bother dropping to my knees at all. I stood bent over, pressing the tissues into the carpet. I heard his chair roll across the floor, and I stood to see what he was doing.

"Are you saying you're not teasing me because you intend to follow through?" He rounded the end of his desk and approached me, and I froze. The game of cat and mouse was exhilarating, but I didn't know if I was actually ready to follow through. Not in his office, anyway. I had thought about it, even had a dirty dream about him last week, but right here, right now?

"I, uh…"

He reached out and rested his hand on my hip, and my body shivered with excitement. I thought we were just flirting a little, some banter, a bit of back and forth. Not this. My tongue stuck to the roof of my mouth. I'd only had sex with one person in my life. I had nothing to offer him, and what if he hated it because I was so inexperienced?

"So you were just teasing me?" His other hand rested on my other hip, and he pulled me against his body. His dick was hard, pressing against my thigh.

"No, sir. I most definitely was not teasing." I licked my lips and rested my hands on his shoulders, tissues conveniently fluttering toward the floor. "I, uh… I just didn't expect you to make a move here, in your office, with Olivia just down the hall."

"No one enters my office unless I invite them in." His eyes devoured me, drinking me in and forcing my blood pressure higher by the second. "And now I'm just waiting for an invitation from you, because I want to be in you."

My vagina ached so badly to let him in. "But sir, we're in your office. The door isn't locked. What if someone knocks?"

"Then we don't answer." His thumbs dug into my hips and his pelvis ground against me.

"You're serious? You want to have sex with me right here? Right now?" I swallowed hard, waiting to hear him say the words.

"Do you want to?" His eyebrows rose, and he stared me in the eyes.

"I… uh…" I licked my lips again. "Yes, I actually do, very much so, sir."

"You like the idea of fucking your boss in his office?"

My heart raced as I found him applying pressure against me, pushing me backward toward the sofa in the corner of his office. I slowly backed up, nearly stumbling when my heel got caught in the same damn spot on the carpet. The shoe came off, and I kicked off the other. He was so much taller than me.

"If I say yes, is that a deal breaker?" I gripped the lapels of his coat as his hands searched the back of my dress for the zipper.

"Hell no. I think it's hot. You be the naughty assistant, and I'll be the demanding boss." He winked, and I felt his hand draw down my back, unzipping the dress and exposing my flesh to the chill of the air-conditioning.

My body was on fire. The banter was so hot, I'd come just from his voice. "Yes, sir." I lowered my arms as he pulled my dress down over my shoulders, and I was thankful I'd worn my good bra to work today. His eyes feasted on my chest, plump, round breasts peeping out of the lacy black bra. "You like what you see, sir?"

"Fuck yes, I do."

I pushed the dress over my hips and let it fall to the floor, taking my panties with it. Daniel tore his suit coat off and undid the fly of his pants. "Sit now," he ordered, and I obeyed. The leather of the sofa was cool on my skin, and I thought for sure Daniel was going to ask me to suck him. So when he dropped to his knees with his hard dick out, ready to fuck me on the edge of the sofa with practiced ease, I wondered how many secretaries he had banged this way.

I spread my legs, and he crawled right up to me, stroking himself as he drooled over my chest. "Want to see more?" I asked him, reaching for my bra clasp, and he nodded. I unhooked it and pushed the straps off my shoulders. It fell behind me on the cushion, and his free hand instantly grabbed my right breast. "Have anything else I can do for you today, sir?"

"Yeah, touch yourself so I can watch."

He knelt there between my knees as I massaged my clit, smearing the body fluids around my soft folds. His hand squeezed my breast harder, then twisted my nipple and pinched it. "Finger yourself," he ordered, so I pushed my fingers into my body while I watched the lust haze form across his eyes. "God, you're hot."

He took a second to pull his shirt off over his head. I expected a man's body, but he had the chest of a god, corded muscles and a complete six-pack. If I kept touching myself like this much longer, I was going to come hard. I moaned slightly when he pushed his pants lower, but when he moved my hand away and teased my pussy with the tip of his cock, I gasped.

"Now, Ms. Kline, I'm going to fuck you, and then you're going to get me new coffee. I'm afraid the other cup has gone cold." His voice was gravelly and rough, but not as rough as the way he forced his dick into me, slamming into my back wall. He wrapped his arms around my body and pulled me toward him as he drove into me. I gasped again.

"Oh, wow…" I moaned, probably a bit too loudly. He shushed me and continued thrusting. My clit, still tender from being touched, rubbed against his pubic bone as his body collided with mine over and over. But it was ten times more intense when he covered my mouth with his and kissed me again.

I gripped Daniel's arms, careful not to use my nails. I didn't want to draw blood and have it stain his shirt when he put it back on, but God, was he huge. I clenched around him and groaned into his mouth as our tongues danced across each other. A deep growl rumbled up his throat, and he bit down on my lower lip. "God, you feel amazing." His kiss became hungrier, devouring me. And I thought he was rough when he first pushed into me, but the longer he fucked me, the harder his thrusts became until he was pounding me so hard the couch shook and bumped on the wall.

"Oh… yes…" I panted and moaned, each of my noises swallowed by his lips. My body was on the edge. I was so close.

"You're a good little assistant, Emily." The hot breath on my face, the growl in his tone, the way he turned into an animal at the sight of my naked body, and I was done. My coil snapped like a rubber band, sending shockwaves through every fiber of my being. I let a wail escape my lips, and Daniel grabbed my hair and pulled my mouth against his harder.

I convulsed around him, at one point having to push him away from my mouth so I could breathe. His hard thrusts continued until I felt him release, spewing hot cum into me. His own grunts mingled with my moans in the song of lovers, and as he slowed, I felt the mess drain out of my body and down the edge of the couch.

"Wow…" I breathed, resting my head on his shoulder. He lingered there, dick still sunk inside me.

"Yeah, wow… God, I've thought of doing that a thousand times since the first day you walked into my office." He let go of my hair and bit my shoulder gently.

"That many times?" I snickered, and he smacked my ass, making a satisfying flesh-on-flesh sound.

"Maybe more." Daniel pulled out and stood. "Stay there," he told me as he walked over to his desk. He took a few tissues out and wiped himself off, then zipped his pants. He brought me the box so I could clean up too.

"Thanks." I wiped the mess up the best I could and tossed the tissues in the bin before collecting our scattered clothing. Daniel watched me the entire time.

"You are gorgeous, you know that?" He took his shirt from me, and I smiled at him.

"I think you've told me that before." I looked everywhere for my bra but couldn't find it, so I dressed without wearing one. The way he watched me made me a bit nervous. "Were you serious about the coffee?"

He chuckled. "Yes, please. I think mine really is cold now. Or maybe I'm too hot after that workout, so the coffee will seem cold."

I zipped myself into the dress and found my shoes. "So… This sort of complicates things, don't you think?" I stood in front of him as he tucked his shirt in and fastened his pants. When he stood up, I thought he would lean in and kiss me, but he patted my arm and strolled to his desk.

"Nothing is complicated." He sat down and straightened a few papers. "Unless you want to make it complicated?" I felt confused by what he said, but he continued so I didn't interrupt. "I think you're amazing, and now I know how good you feel, so that's not complicated to me."

He'd said the word complicated so many times, it was beginning to not sound like a word at all. I also felt a little cold, not intimate and close to him the way I thought I would feel after that. Maybe he was still playing the naughty banter game we had started before the sex, or maybe he had zero intentions of actually dating me. It was just sex with my boss.

I let the thought remain in my head for a second but knew if I hung out there too long with it on my mind, I'd regret it.

"Let me go get that coffee for you, sir."

"Daniel... please." The way he looked at me told me it was not just sex with my boss, so that added to my confusion.

"Daniel," I repeated.

As I walked down the hallway, my mind was a whirlwind of thoughts. He was incredible in every way. I had no mirror to check my appearance and I just knew someone heard our sex. I wanted so much more with him, but I wasn't sure he wanted it too, or what he wanted, for that matter.

And we hadn't used protection.

That was a huge mistake.

6

DANIEL

"Yes, and I shot par two weeks ago in Malibu. It was fantastic. Not such an easy course, though." Dad wiped the sweat from his forehead for the third time in ten minutes.

The sun overhead was warm. It was a perfect day for a tee-time with Dad. I stood next to his limo, chatting with him as his driver loaded my clubs into the trunk. We had a routine of playing nine holes at least once a month. Traffic was light, which meant a quick commute, and I should be back to the office to finish off the last few filings before close of business.

"That's fantastic. You know, I've not had much time to work on my game, so you'll put me to shame out there for sure." He laughed at me, but I knew why. He always put me to shame. Dad should have joined the pro circuit. He was that good. Meanwhile, I was a hobby golfer. I had other things I enjoyed doing much more than golf, so I never took it that seriously.

"Sir!" At the call, I turned to see Emily jogging toward me. The way her dress fit a bit looser in the top without her bra on had me ogling her once again. Her chest swayed as she approached, and I wanted to see those tits bouncing again. "Sir, you left your gloves on your desk. I was just preparing the files for faxing and I found them."

Winded, she handed me the gloves and smiled politely at my father. His eyebrows rose in intrigue. I couldn't help myself. She was too alluring, her body too tempting. I took the gloves from her and said, "You let me forget things like that again and I'll have to bend you over my desk, Ms. Kline." No one was around us except my father. He wouldn't say anything to anyone, and his smirk told me he appreciated a little office flirtation.

"Uh… I…" Emily seemed nervous.

"What's wrong? Cat got your tongue? Or are you imagining it wrapped around my cock?" I had no clue what had come over me, except that the feeling of being buried inside her this morning had me entirely entranced. She was that amazing.

She tried to hide her grin as she looked down, but she didn't shy away. "No, sir. I was just thinking next time we should lock the door, that's all." Her eyes flicked nervously at my father, who shook his head and climbed into the limo at the driver's behest.

"I gotta run. Tee-time." I had the urge to lean over and kiss her, but I restrained myself. While staffers in the office may not be able to hear our banter, they would definitely see me kiss her should they be looking out the window. "Sorry if I embarrassed you in front of my father. He's a good sport, won't tell a soul."

"It's okay. Go have fun. I'll have your filings ready when you get back." She crossed her arms over her chest and backed away. "But I was serious about locking the door next time. Might want some loud music too so I can scream your name." She winked and turned, walking away with that ass swaying with every step.

I laughed for a moment at her cheeky behavior and climbed into the limo. For a small town girl, she had sass and I liked it. Every new thing I learned about her, I loved. Emily had no idea how hard I was falling for her, and I wanted to tell the world.

"A little hanky-panky in the office, huh?" Dad asked as I buckled my seatbelt and the limo pulled into traffic. "I did a bit of that in my day too." He winked at me and nodded approvingly.

"Ah, this is no hanky-panky, Pop. Emily is something special. I really like her. And the best part is she's just as bold as I am." I thought about how she seductively knelt on the ground with her ass in the air for me to admire it.

"She's a new partner? Bringing your gloves to you like an assistant?" His eyes narrowed in suspicion, so I put that suspicion to bed right away.

"Oh, no. She is an assistant, and she's very good at her job." I watched out the window as we passed a line of traffic moving slower than us. Dad's line of questioning was pretty normal for anyone I dated. He thought every woman was beneath me.

"You're taking a serious interest in someone who is a mere assistant? Not even a paralegal? Does she even have an education?" I didn't like his tone at all, but I knew better than to question him or go against what he thought. I lived my life very happily on my own until my parents stuck their nose in my business.

"She has a degree, Pop. She's a wonderful woman." I had nothing negative to say about Emily at all, and I wasn't going to stoop to arguing with him over her socio-economic status.

The car fell silent, and I turned to my phone, scrolling my latest notifications. Neither of us spoke again until we had checked in and were driving to the first hole on the golf cart. We weaved through the thick pines on the path. The man drove too fast, causing me to grip the handle tightly.

"I was thinking of having lunch with you and Mom, maybe Nick too. What do you think?" I thought breaking the tension between us with a change of subject would be good, but Dad sat on the topic of Emily like he was king of the mountain.

"So you can bring your assistant?" His tone was dry. He was trying to get a rise out of me, which I wouldn't give him.

"It would be nice to introduce her to Mom, yes." The caddy stopped and turned the cart off and headed for our clubs while Dad and I donned our gloves and waited.

"You know, it's one thing to have a little fling with a woman beneath your status. Lots of women are gorgeous and put out a little." He took the seven-iron handed to him by the caddy. I rolled my eyes at him. "It's another thing entirely to lower your standards to date someone who isn't even in the same tax bracket. Paralegal, maybe—they have a shot at becoming a lawyer one day. But a mere assistant?"

Dad strutted up to the tee and balanced his ball on it. I'd have rather ignored the topic the rest of the day and just enjoyed golf, but I knew he wouldn't let up. It was now a game of how long I could remain patient with him before I snapped. He took the swing and his ball sailed down the fairway, then he stepped aside and gestured for me to approach. The caddy handed me a seven-iron and a ball, and I took my stance. But when I took my swing, Dad started in again, and the ball sliced to the right into the rough.

"Seriously, Daniel. We raised you better than that. The best private schools. You went to Harvard, for Christ's sake. You can't date an assistant."

I clenched my jaw and thrust the club toward the caddy who looked a bit frightened, but he took the clubs and headed for the cart. Pretending I hadn't heard Dad's comment, I climbed onto the cart and held on tightly as Dad climbed in next to me and the caddy took off.

"She's just out for your money. You wait and see. She's going to do something stupid like file a lawsuit for harassment, or maybe she'll tell you her car broke down and get you to buy her a new one. Women like that don't belong in our circle, Daniel."

"Dad, can you just lay off? Please?" I snapped like a twig. "I just want to enjoy golf, okay? You've made your point."

He fell silent, but I knew it wasn't the end of it. He'd bring it up again later on and badger me about it. Strange how they did the same thing to Nick, my younger brother, but when he'd moved on to marry his now wife, Ginny, they'd been forced to accept her into the family. I didn't feel I'd be that lucky.

The rest of the afternoon dragged by. We talked very little, focusing the conversation we did have on the task at hand. I wasn't surprised to double bogey most of the holes. Dad played almost a perfect game, making note very loudly in the clubhouse afterward. All I could do was be grateful he wasn't still harping on me for dating Emily.

By the time I got back to the office, Emily had gone for the day and

I was exhausted. I had planned to ask her to chat with me about what happened this morning. After Michael's lectures, I figured we had to discuss the difficult dynamic of my being her boss and how that could be misinterpreted on either part. A seed of doubt needled at my thoughts after Dad's rant about her, but I'd managed to push that away. I didn't think for a second that Emily was just out for my money. I was the one who had made the advances on her first. Not the other way around.

Still, communication is a foundation for all relationships and I wanted to start this one off right with a clear idea of her expectations and my boundaries. I sat behind my desk, unable to focus on the filings and faxes simply because all I could think about was seeing her tomorrow morning. In fact, I decided right then to ask Olivia to make Emily my full-time assistant, not sharing her time with any other partner. I wanted to see her as much as possible.

7

EMILY

The waiter with his dark, curly hair took our empty plates away after asking if we wanted dessert. The posh restaurant Evelyn chose for our evening out probably wasn't as ritzy as I thought it was, but back in Monroe County, the fanciest restaurant we had was a McDonald's and it was always busy. Here in Chicago, to eat at a joint like this was probably beneath some people, but to me it was fine dining.

"You ought to give him your number," Evelyn prodded, elbowing me. I sat on her side of the booth, unable to get out without her moving first. Charlotte sat across from us, snickering. Both of them liked to set me up with guys they thought I'd be good with. I couldn't count how many times I'd had to cancel a blind date they wanted me to go on.

"No, I don't like him. Guys, he's too young. He looks straight out of high school." I gulped the glass of wine and shook my head. I wasn't really into younger guys at all, but the prospect of an older guy had never turned me away.

"Alright, well what about the guy at the bar?" Evelyn continued her sisterly badgering. Being married now, she insisted that I was missing out on something amazing. She had a toddler and a nice little domestic life, whereas I was still single and ready to mingle.

Charlotte, being engaged, egged Evelyn on most days, though she was always more supportive of my singlehood. She rolled her eyes at Evelyn's prodding and being my best friend, she stood up for me. "Look, Eve, if she's not ready to date, she's not ready."

"I didn't say I'm not ready." I set my wine glass down and felt heat creeping into my cheeks. The thought of Daniel and me dating had been on my mind for days now. After sex with him last week, he was all I could think about. I'd even made a few mistakes at work and Olivia had to scold me for being distracted, but how was I supposed to focus on boring paperwork and filing briefs when Daniel was just down the hall?

"Oh, yeah? So the guy, at the bar, with the tattoo." Evelyn pointed a thumb over her shoulder, and I turned to see a man there. What Evelyn failed to notice was the ring on his left ring finger.

"Married." I shrugged and finished my wine. "Besides, I think I might be into someone at work."

"Ooh," Charlotte called, leaning in. Her eyebrows waggled as she said, "Tell me now. All the details."

I grinned, not sure how to explain exactly what was happening between me and Daniel because we hadn't even talked about it yet. We'd had lunch multiple times and chatted, then flirted a lot. The sex was completely out of left field and had my mind reeling, but it was amazing and I wanted it again. Still, there was no evidence that he wanted a relationship. The most encouragement I'd gotten was his naughty flirting before golf the day we'd had sex. Since then, he'd been busy.

"I don't know what there is to say."

"Uh, hello? Everything?" Evelyn angled her body to face me and poked me on the shoulder. "Who is he? What is his job? What does he look like? What's his name?"

Charlotte slurped her soda and nodded along with Evelyn's interrogation. "Yes, all of those details and more. We want to know how you met, and what you've done with him. Have you gone to dinner? Lunch? Kissed?"

I regretted opening my mouth at all. Both of them were incorrigible, honestly, and I knew they would never let me out of the booth until I'd spilled the beans. I took a deep breath, sighed, and started my story.

"So, his name is Daniel. He's a little older than me, and he's really handsome. Uh, he's a lawyer, and I met him the first day because I assist him sometimes with paperwork and stuff." I eyed Evelyn as she took out her phone and started typing. I thought maybe she was texting her husband or something, so I continued. "Anyway, I brought him some files one day and he had extra lunch. He asked me to sit and eat with him. He's so amazing, Char. He plays basketball and loves sports. He's a reader too. Gosh, we have so much in common." I heard myself swooning over the details.

"Oh, he sounds amazing. How romantic. You had lunch with him? What else? Has he taken you to dinner? Have you kissed him?"

At Charlotte's question, I found my cheeks burning, just thinking of how little kissing we accomplished before we had sex, and then the kissing was only to keep me from making so much noise the whole office would hear. I swore Olivia was suspicious as I walked past her office on the way to the bathroom to wash my face and check my hair. And Grace had given me the stink eye too.

"Uh, well…" I was nervous. I'd tell Charlotte anything, but with Evelyn there, I was intimidated. She always told Mom everything, even things that were none of Mom's business.

"You kissed him!" Charlotte snickered. "You little vixen. Oh, my gosh, is he a good kisser?" She leaned in, eyes wide in suspense as I hesitated to answer her. I was anxious about what she'd say, but more so what Evelyn would say.

Shrugging, I bit my lower lip and gave her a knowing look, not turning my eyes away from her. I hoped she would understand that I'd had sex with him, not just kissed him, but without telling Evelyn about it. At least not yet. Her eyebrows rose, eyes widening, and she gasped. "No way! Really?" She leaned forward, palms splayed on the table.

I grinned and looked down. That's when Evelyn finally chimed in, oblivious to the interaction between me and Charlotte. She had a scowl on her face that reminded me exactly of my mother and took the wind out of my sails instantly.

"Are you talking about Daniel Jacobs? The head partner and CEO?" Evelyn stared at me, phone in hand with damning evidence. She was on the company site, scrolling the headshots of all the lawyers on staff. Daniel was the only "Dan" who worked there. "Emily, you realize he's twelve years older than you, right? He could be your father."

I snatched her phone away from her and locked it, laying it on the table. I was frustrated that she couldn't just be happy for me. "You're ridiculous. Twelve-year-olds don't have sex, and if they did, they don't get women pregnant. Okay? He's not old enough to be my father."

"That's a huge age gap. What is wrong with guys your age? And the head partner? He's probably just sexually harassing you and you're too naïve to know that." Evelyn turned to Charlotte. "Tell her it's gross."

Charlotte shook her head. "No, it's not gross, but it is sort of odd. I mean, is he nice? Like, does he talk to you like a human? Evelyn has a point, Em. What if he's just using his authority to pressure you into sex?"

"Oh, believe me," I told them, "he doesn't have to make me do anything." I had to hide the smirk on my face. "I'm very willing to do anything he wants to."

Evelyn remained quiet, now clutching the phone in her hand again. The way she retreated into herself when Charlotte hadn't agreed with her was concerning, but at least she wasn't badgering me anymore. I turned to Charlotte and sighed, ignoring Evelyn's glower.

"Anyway, we have so much in common and I think we really like each other. I want to see where it goes. I know it's not conventional to date someone so much older than me, but he's got his life together, which is more than I can say for most men my own age."

"Well, I say be careful. That's all." Charlotte finished her soda and waved the waiter over to our table. "Just use your brain, not your hormones. If he tells you that you have to do something with him to keep your job, then it's definitely harassment. Got it?"

I nodded in agreement, and Evelyn excused herself to use the toilet before we left. We all came separately, so I didn't worry about being lectured more in the car, though I was concerned Evelyn would run straight to my parents with the juicy gossip and they'd call me with their concerned parent act.

After we paid and said goodbye, I walked toward the metro line which would take me to my apartment. Daniel hadn't pressured me at all. I thought I was the one who'd instigated things, which I knew would bring up a whole other level of gossip if people found out. Evelyn would assume, like my coworkers, that I was trying to sleep my way to the top, when in fact, I had no interest in climbing that ladder. I wanted to use my degree in business to help a company really grow, not stick around a law firm. I'd never be a partner, and that was what I wanted, to be at the top.

I swiped my metro pass and found a seat on the train taking me home, and my phone buzzed. I reached into my pocket to see a call from an unknown number had been missed, then a text came in as I was checking my notifications.

Unknown sender 9:17 PM: Your tits are so perfect, I want to suck them.

I read the message and froze. Who on earth could be sending me nasty things like this? I looked around the car as it started moving and covered my phone so people around me didn't see it, and the phone buzzed again. I looked down to see another message.

Unknown sender 9:18 PM: If I send you my address, will you come over so I can bury my cock inside you?

This one was worse than the previous one. It made me tremble to think someone had this number, or maybe it was just a prank, I didn't know. I typed a message into the phone and hit *Send* as quickly as I could, then blocked the number immediately.

Emily 9:19 PM: Sorry. I'm taken already. Lose my number.

I sat back on the train, nervous. Very few people had my number at all, and I had no idea who it could be. The entire train ride, I felt hypervigilant, studying the faces of people around me on the train as if by examining them, I may discover who it was that had messaged me. I feared someone was following me too, so I called Charlotte to chat with her just to calm my nerves. The topic of Evelyn came up, though, which soured the chat.

"You think she's going to make a fuss, call your mom like she normally does?" I could hear Charlotte eating again and wondered how she ate so much and stayed so thin.

"Yes, I absolutely think she will. It's only a matter of time before my mom calls me to lecture me." The train pulled into my station, and I rose and made my way off the train and up the stairs toward the exit.

"Gosh, well I'm here for you. I'm happy you met someone, and I really hope he's not a loser. I hope it works out." I could always count on my best friend to have my back.

"Thanks, Char. I'm going to go now. I'm just about to my place. Thanks for keeping me company."

"You got it, babe. Call if you need me again."

As I pushed the elevator call button, I resolved that I had to talk to Daniel about whatever this was that we were doing. I liked him a lot, and I wanted more than just office lunches and sex. I wanted to see where it went because I saw us having a real shot at something special. Besides, he wasn't my direct supervisor. Olivia was. How could that affect my job?

8

DANIEL

I held down the button on the intercom, calling Jill, who responded immediately.

"Yes, sir?"

Chipper as always, her voice rang through the line clear. "Jill, I need you to get Olivia and come to my office, please."

"Of course, sir."

I leaned back in my chair, reflecting on the decision I had made. Emily was perfect as an assistant, but I wanted more time with her. Just seeing that couch where she and I had sex now more than ten days ago was a huge reminder of just how much I liked her company. We still hadn't discussed the encounter due to my busy schedule, but we had fallen into a comfortable rhythm with work. She brought me coffee just the way I liked it, and I invited her to lunch daily. Twice, she spent her lunch hour with coworkers instead of me, which I encouraged in the name of her building relationships within the firm.

Now I waited for her boss to come and hear my new directions. The clock on the wall ticked seconds by, frustrating me that Olivia was taking so long to come at my call. Jill would have been here in a few seconds, but I gave Olivia the benefit of the doubt. As partner, she was likely busy with a client, which is the only reason I would have considered worthy of making me wait. Everyone knew I was a hard man to please, Emily included.

When the soft knock came at the door, I called, "Come in." Both Jill and Olivia knew to knock and wait for my call, which is something Emily would never do now because I'd given her free reign of my office.

"Sir, you needed to see me?"

"Both of you, yes." Olivia nodded at my correction, and both women approached my desk. Jill had a pleasant look on her face, but Olivia looked perplexed, so I cut to the chase. "Tell me what you know about Emily Kline."

Olivia's brow furrowed and she glanced at Jill. "Well, Emily graduated magna cum laude from UC Berkeley with a master's in business management. She was near the top of her class. She grew up in Monroe County, Illinois, in a small town. She has a small family and is new to the city."

I could have known that all on my own. What I was interested in was tidbits about Emily she'd share with a coworker that she might not feel comfortable sharing with her boss, the CEO. "I've read her resume, Olivia. I mean, you've gotten to know her a bit. What is she like?"

"Uh, sir, we had lunch a few times so far," Jill chimed in with a smile. "Emily is generous, and she has a mothering sort of attitude and wants to make sure everyone is taken care of and happy. She brings me a coffee every morning, and she makes sure to order it how I like it."

"Ah, that's good to know." I thought she'd only done that for me, but I liked that she was as kind to everyone as she was to me. Though that brought some doubts to mind that her kindness toward me was more than just at a coworker level, and given her response to my text messages a few nights ago, I worried maybe she really was seeing someone else. "Go on."

"Sir," Olivia started, "she is prompt. She is detail oriented with a laser focus. When I ask her to do something, she exceeds my expectations regularly. I agree with Jill. She is generous and thoughtful. I also think she is very ambitious, but not in the way you might think."

This I already knew, but I'd let them tell me.

"Yes, she told me she wants to use this job as a stepping stone, a personal experience builder to help her resume. She wants to really build a career around business strategy and consulting." Jill wrung her hands and eyed me nervously. "Why do you ask, sir?"

"Well, I have a proposition." I stood and buttoned my suit coat, realizing I hadn't stood when they entered the room the way I always did when Emily walked in. It was evidence to me that I saw her differently at my core level, not just because she was gorgeous. "Jill, you are now going to be office management. You will oversee both Emily and Olivia's secretary, Brita. The rest of the assistants and office staffers too. It's a bump in pay, and a reduction in hours, allowing you to spend more time with your children without lacking finances."

Jill's eyes lit up. "What? I'm getting a promotion?" She hadn't seen a promotion in the years she'd worked for me, so it was a long time coming. Besides, I knew she could really do more with her talents.

"Yes." I nodded and turned to Olivia, too ready to be down to business to revel in her excitement. "Olivia, Emily is now my permanent assistant. Call her a secretary or whatever. It doesn't matter. If we need another assistant, talk to HR to find a good salary range and start hunting."

"But, sir, I hardly got Emily settled in." I met Olivia's protest with a raised hand. She stopped talking, but her face said so many things her lips couldn't utter. She was upset with me.

"My decision is final. I'll have you send her in now too, so I can give her the news. Also, tell Gary in HR to bump Emily's salary and Jill's, both by ten percent. Got it?"

Olivia offered a skeptical look and pursed her lips. "Yes, sir."

"Thank you, Mr. Jacobs," Jill said, now almost giddy. She turned and followed Olivia out, shutting the door behind herself, and I sat back down, ready to enact part two of my plan. I wanted to have Emily in this office as much as possible, even if it meant cutting into my own profits as the head of this firm.

Trying to get my mind focused on work, I flicked through a few case briefings on my computer while I waited for Emily to come in. It wasn't like her to keep me waiting, so when nearly twenty minutes had passed and she barged in a bit flustered, I was surprised. She looked like a scolded puppy, but rather than focusing on her emotional reaction, I focused on how out of character this was for her. Even Olivia had mentioned how prompt Emily was.

"I asked for you to come in here more than twenty minutes ago." I stood and greeted her, gesturing for her to sit in one of the chairs at the table across the room.

"Sorry, Olivia had a few things for me to finish up at the last minute, and she wanted to talk to me too." She pulled a chair out and sat down, smoothing the flyaways around her temples and tucking them behind her ear. "What did you need, sir?"

"First of all, stop calling me sir." I chuckled as I sat down, which drew a smile to her lips. "And second of all, you're going to be my personal assistant permanently now."

She offered a confused but happy expression. "I'm what?"

"Yes, my personal assistant alone. No one else in the firm gets to access that amazing talent you have. Got it? So when you report to work tomorrow morning, you can clean out your old desk and move into Jill's." She opened her mouth to protest, but I forestalled her complaints. "I've given Jill a promotion."

"You did that just so I could report only to you?" Her hand fluttered to her chest where she toyed with a small gold charm on the necklace she wore. It drew my eyes to the dip in her blouse and the hint of cleavage showing.

"I did." I licked my lips, ready to taste her skin, but we needed to talk first. "And there is something I've been meaning to discuss with you for a while." My dick was swelling, the skin feeling tight already. She did that to me—aroused me like no woman I'd ever met.

"What's that?" Emily relaxed into the chair and tilted her head at me.

"The way your pussy felt wrapped around my cock."

As I said the words, I watched her visibly tense. She sat straighter, her eyebrows rose, and she glanced at the door. "I hardly think that's appropriate conversation for a workplace."

"Then you're really going to think what I have to say next is inappropriate." I saw the grin she tried to hide. "I really like you, and I want you to consider what we might have together."

"Meaning?" she asked, toying with her necklace again. Her lips darkened by several shades, and I sensed she was eager for me to clarify.

"I mean, when you find someone you click with instantly, and you feel like you've known them your whole life, you just know it's right. You fit with them, like peanut butter and jelly, or mashed potatoes and gravy. And you, Emily, are my perfect match."

"Sir, I…" She looked down, smiling.

"I said stop calling me sir. My name is Daniel. You can call me Dan, or Danny, or even D, but please do not be so professional with me anymore. I meant it when I said I like you."

Emily's face remained downturned, but the smile she had didn't escape me. She was timid but not weak, polite, but not a pushover. I studied her while she considered my words, the way her hair fell in soft waves around her face, the way the curve of her breasts was provocative, yet modest in their own way. Emily wasn't a shark like Olivia and Grace, but she wasn't a limp noodle like some of the other assistants I'd had. And she had some fight in her, a spirit to strive for excellence even if she was going against the grain. I noticed that the first time she walked right into my office without knocking.

"I'm not sure how to respond right now." Her cheeks were tinged pink—embarrassment or shyness—but her lips grew darker. That meant arousal.

I leaned forward and grabbed her hand, bringing it to my lips to kiss it. "Say nothing right now." Her palms were sweaty, another sign that she was nervous, but I was about to put her so at ease, she wouldn't be able to walk when I was done with her.

She looked up at me, mouth held slightly open. "But…"

"Just go lock the door."

9

EMILY

I did as he asked, locking the door. The minute he asked me to do it, my body responded. I knew what he wanted, and I'd been aching for it too. I stood by the locked door, a bit more at ease this time than I was last time. He held his hand in the air, curling a finger and drawing me closer to him.

"The door is locked, sir. What now?" I played with the button on my dress. My core throbbed, moisture already puddling between my legs in anticipation of his touch. And the lust in his eyes taunted me, forcing my body to slick itself against the fabric of my panties.

I glanced at the windows. He'd already drawn the shades. He sat watching me move closer, and I could see his thumb rubbing across the front of his slacks. "Take your clothes off."

A promotion and a locked door, and now this? My gut roiled for a moment, hesitating. I questioned his motives in my head. He didn't need to use his authority to pull strings for me to get time to do this because I wanted it as much as he clearly did. But he had, or maybe it only looked like he had. But from his own lips, he made it clear to me that he wanted me all to himself and that was why he'd given me this job. I just stared at him blankly as I pondered what to do.

"Your clothes, now, Ms. Kline." His finger flicked in the air, pointing at me, then the floor. "I'm not waiting."

I couldn't tell if he was just playing the naughty boss-employee game we engaged in last time or if he really was just throwing his proverbial weight around. Ambivalence won out, and I froze.

"Look, Emily, I think I made it clear just before that I'm not just interested in sex with you." He stood and walked over to me, seeming to understand my internal conflict. "I really like you, and I want to spend more time with you to get to know you as a person because what I know so far is so amazing, I'm willing to jump through hoops and upset my parents just to have it."

I grinned and looked down as he held my shoulders. "If you don't want to do this, we don't have to. We'll just talk."

"No," I blurted, biting my lip. "I mean, no, sir."

"Well then, take your clothes off like I told you."

All of my indecision vanished, and I started peeling the layers off. When I stood in front of him in just my bra and panties, he shook his head. "All of it," he said, unbuckling his fly.

My vagina screamed at me. This was insane, the level to which I would go to please this man, but God, did I want to. I would have done anything he asked in that moment and Evelyn would have called that a weakness, but I called it prowess. I shimmied my hips, sliding my silky panties until they dropped to the floor, and then undid my bra.

Daniel helped out of the bra, tossing it to the side, then pointed at his desk, conveniently cleared of anything that might hinder our having a good time. "Bend over," he ordered. He had his cock in hand, stroking it. I was a little disappointed that he didn't want to kiss me first, but when he pulled a handkerchief out of his pocket and dangled it in front of me, I understood what he wanted.

"Uh... no." I shook my head. "You're not tying my mouth." I chuckled. I might have been a bit green, but I was not naïve. Some sexual practices were just outside my comfort zone.

"No... not going to gag you. Just offering something to bite on to muffle the sounds you're going to make. Last time, we were lucky and it was early. This time, there are lots of people behind that door and you cannot be heard. Do you understand me?" His eyes were serious. I nodded.

"Yes, sir." I took the handkerchief and twisted it, wrapping it around my fist.

"Then bend over and spread yourself because you're getting fucked, Ms. Kline."

I smirked at him and bent over his desk. With one hand, I reached behind me and spread myself open for him. He stood stroking himself looking at me, and I watched him over my shoulder. "Like what you see, sir?"

"Hell yes, I do."

Daniel advanced on me with tiger eyes. He slid his dick up and down my slit, spreading my moisture. Then he pushed into me, and I groaned loudly.

"Shh..." he hissed, reminding me that this session had to be silent. I remembered the handkerchief twisted and wrapped around my knuckles, and I brought my hand to my mouth and bit down, letting my whimpers of pleasure be absorbed by the soft cotton. "Good girl," he whispered. "Now tell me you want me to fuck you."

"I want you to fuck me."

"Ah... but you forgot something."

"I want you to fuck me, sir." I whimpered and stuffed my fist back against my face, biting down hard. My pussy clenched and squeezed him. He felt amazing sliding in and out of me. The friction was incredible, and I already felt like he was going to make me come. I'd never had an orgasm from only internal stimulation. I wanted to reach for my clit, but his firm hand pinned me to the desk, leaving no room for me to touch myself.

"God, your ass is perfect," he mumbled, but I heard him. He thrust harder, driving me against the desk. I'd definitely have bruises from how my hips ground against the hardwood, but I didn't care.

"Oh, God..." I moaned into the fabric. I grabbed the edge of the desk and rocked my hips upward. It put his cock in the perfect position to hit my back wall and drive me mad with lust. "Oh, God..." I groaned again, louder than I should have.

Daniel reached up and grabbed a handful of my hair and pulled my head back at an angle. "I said, be quiet, Ms. Kline." His voice wasn't loud, but it was commanding, and the tone he took—of authority and assertiveness—made my body tremble with desire.

"Yes, sir," I muttered, and he let my hair go. I pressed my hand against my mouth again and clenched around him, and as I did I felt my orgasm creep in on me. "Now..." I whispered. "Now... please..."

He thrust faster, and it was enough. My body convulsed, and I could do nothing about it but make sure my mouth was covered. The whimpers and bleats of enjoyment were mostly muffled by the hand-kerchief, and I was glad he'd given it to me. He made me feel incredible again, and if he wanted to keep going, I'd have three or four more orgasms.

But I felt him explode inside me, then his cum running down my leg. His body was made for mine—the way he brought me to climax so quickly and made sure I was pleased before he let himself enjoy it. He slid out of me, and more cum dribbled from me. I was legless, draped over the desk, unable to move for a moment. I heard his belt jingle, then I felt his hands on my thighs, drying his mess off me.

I pushed myself off the desk and turned to face him. He tossed the tissues and handed me my clothes, which I took from him with a hazy half-grin. "Does that mean we're an item now, then?"

"I'm not going to deny the opportunity exists." I liked how his eyes drank me in even after his lust was sated and he had no reason to look at me like a hungry animal. "But I do have something for you."

He walked around his desk and opened a drawer as I dressed quickly. I half expected it to be my bra which I lost last time, and I made sure to put every item of clothing I'd worn in back on this time. When he handed me a business card, I was confused.

"I know where you work." I snickered and took the card.

"Turn it over," he said, pointing, so I did.

I read the hand-scrawled number on the back of the card. It was very familiar to me, but I couldn't place it immediately. I assumed it was his cell number, and it made me happy to know he was serious about having a real relationship, not just sex at work.

"If you have a boyfriend, you need to break up with him. You're mine now."

The way he said that so possessively supercharged my body. I got a rush out of his claiming me. "Uh, I'm not seeing anyone at all. Why would you think that?"

"Well, I texted you the other day. Got your number from our personnel files, and you told me that you were taken." He leaned against the edge of his desk, where I had just been bent across it. "So, if you're taken, get rid of him."

I chuckled and shook my head. "I didn't know it was you. I thought my sister gave my number to a creepy guy or something. I was talking about you."

Daniel's eyebrows rose in surprise. "You were?"

"Yeah... I can't seem to think about anyone but you lately. It even distracts me from work at times. I told you that." I slid the card into my bra and straightened my top before tossing my hair to make sure it looked unfussed.

"I'm flattered." He reached out and took my hand. "You really want to give this a go?"

"Yes, Dan. I really do."

"I'm way older than you."

"I don't care." I took a step toward him. "Age is just a number."

"And I'm your boss."

"And I'm falling in love with you. What does that matter? When lightning strikes, you absorb it and let it charge the atmosphere. You don't run from it."

He leaned forward and kissed me gently, lingering for a moment. "Okay, then. I guess any woman who turns other men away because she wants me even before she knows how I feel is a woman I want to get to know more." His lips brushed mine again. "Because I may just be falling for her too."

My heart soared. He had no idea what that confession did to me. I wanted to stay there and talk, but I knew work was calling.

"We should…" I pointed my thumb over my shoulder.

"We should," he said resolutely. "But your lunches are mine now. And when I message you, don't tell me to buzz off again." He winked at me, and I chuckled, leaving him there at his desk.

Things just got a whole lot more interesting, and I was walking on air. I'd tell Charlotte everything, but Evelyn would just have to hear it through the grapevine. I was falling in love.

10

DANIEL

I watched Emily saunter out of my office tugging at the hem of her skirt. She fluffed her hair and stepped into the hallway and I relaxed behind my desk. The storm that walked into my office, however, was one I wasn't expecting.

My mother's head jerked back and forth worse than a bobble head on the dashboard of a 1970s Volkswagen van. She scoffed and huffed, pointing in the direction Emily was moving. "You have got to be kidding me." Mom stood there staring down the hall, and I had to restrain myself from rolling my eyes at her ridiculous dramatic response.

"What, Mom?" I sat forward in my chair, resting my forearms on the edge of the desk and clasping my hands. The room smelled like sex, and I didn't care. It was my office, my firm, and my business.

She whipped around and shut the door behind her before stomping to my desk and slamming her purse down. Her nostrils were flared out and her eyes narrowed. "I can't believe he was telling the truth. I had to come see it for myself." Standing with her hands on her hips, she glared at me the way she did when I was a naughty child, but she had to know that wasn't going to work anymore.

"See what?" I gestured at the chair for her to sit, and she flopped into it dramatically.

"That two-bit floozy your father told me about. An assistant, Daniel?" She leaned in as she hissed out the words. "You can do so much better."

"Please don't talk about Emily like that, Mom. You don't know the first thing about her." My temper bristled at her insults. I wanted to be respectful as always, but I had to draw the line somewhere. My parents meddled in my life far too much.

Mom huffed again, sitting back on her chair and crossing her arms over her chest defiantly. Her red, pinstripe suit buckled in the front, leaving wrinkles, which normally would have annoyed her. Today, it appeared as if I annoyed her more than wrinkled clothing. She crossed one leg over the other and bounced her foot hard.

"I want what's best for you, Daniel. Any mother would want what's best for their child. I just don't know why you insist on lowering your standards so low. An assistant? Really? I mean, is she in law school?"

"No, Mom, she's not. She is brilliant and kind, and if you took even two seconds to get to know her, you'd see for yourself that she is pretty perfect for me."

"Because she's easy? What did you do, bend her over the desk?" Her tone was nasty, and it was difficult to remain calm. I refused to respond to her question, which didn't faze her. She kept right on with her insults. "Her hair was fussed, her skirt riding up. This whole room smells like sex. You can't lie to me. I'm your mother. You are purposely destroying your career."

"Mom!" I snapped without raising my voice, but if she didn't stop what she was doing, she would see my claws come out. "Please, we can talk about this and be civil. Emily has done nothing wrong. She is a good girl."

"Girl! Ha. See? Even you admit she's just a child. What will the media say when they find out you're dating a child? Hm?" Her eyebrows rose in accusation, and she gestured wildly with her hand. "This whole thing will be over. You'll lose everything. She'll get wind that you have as much money as you have and file a lawsuit for sexual harassment. The media will pick it up and call you a pedophile or something. Daniel, listen to me. End it now."

Mom picked up her purse and opened it, rifling through it. She pulled out a bottle of pills and took two of them then put the bottle back. She didn't even use water to wash them down. I wasn't sure if they were anxiety pills or just medicine for a headache. Maybe she took them as a means to make me feel guilty, like my actions had spurred her into some frenzied state she couldn't control.

I wished I had a bottle of tequila to drown out the anger roiling around my gut, but even if I had it, I'd have passed on it. I had important meetings this afternoon that I couldn't screw up. Dealing with my mother wasn't ever easy, but this interaction was really pushing my buttons in a bad way.

"Look, I know you care, but you are way out of your realm of authority."

"Am I?" She glared at me. "I think your dating a gold-digging whore is sort of my realm of authority. We made you everything you are. Let me remind you who paid for your college? Who invested in this firm to get you started? Who got you on the right track with your first cases and—"

"I get it, Mom. You and Dad sacrificed a lot to get me here, and I appreciate that. But my career is separate from my personal life. Dating Emily is not going to tank my career." I had to take a deep breath to keep from shouting at her, though I really wanted to let loose.

Mom bolted out of her seat, pacing the length of the room. She simply didn't understand where I was coming from because she hadn't even spoken to Emily. Neither of my parents even wanted to. They'd just as soon make their quick judgments and write her off as not good enough for me because she didn't have a name or a reputation.

"You know, Daniel, I thought I taught you better than this. Think of what your clients will do when they see you dating someone so young? You think that's just a threat? What about Bob Nickles? His daughter was preyed upon by an older man who nearly brainwashed her into joining a cult. How will you explain to him why you're so obsessed with her? And she works for you!"

Mom was seething, eyes bulging out of her head, hands clenched into fists. "What if your other staff members see you as playing favorites and start expecting you to do things for them the way you do for her? Hm? When you don't do it, they'll file a lawsuit against you for preferential treatment or uneven working conditions."

"Mom, please sit down. This is ridiculous." I stood, pressing the tips of my fingers into my desk. Mom sat on the couch angrily and leaned back. As she did, she fidgeted a bit until she reached behind herself and pulled out Emily's black lace bra. I remembered peeling that thing off her and letting it fall. I hadn't even realized it was lost in the furniture.

"My God, Daniel." She shook her head and dropped the bra, covering her face. "You can't possibly be doing this to me."

There it was, the hard eye roll. Everything in my mother's life was about her, including who I chose to date. I could already hear the next phrase out of her mouth before she opened it. The ladies at her rotary club were going to have a tizzy. The men at Dad's cigar club were going to tout me as the king of the hill, big man on campus for scoring such a hottie, all to his obvious disdain. And I was the black sheep, bleating out the family shame at the top of my lungs.

"Daniel, I—"

"I know, Mom. Your friends. Dad's friends. Etcetera, etcetera." I waved my hand in the air and strolled over to her, bringing her purse along with me. I handed it to her and snatched Emily's bra up. "Look, I understand your concern, but I want you to know I'm not going to ruin my life. I know what I'm doing. I really like this woman." Careful not to call Emily a "girl" again, I thrust a hand out and helped her stand. "Now I have work to do, which if I don't get it done will actually tank my career. So if you have anything else to say about my personal life, maybe it can wait until I'm on personal time."

Mom fussed with me, grinding her foot into the carpet as if she were not leaving, but I opened the door and stood there waiting for her. "Daniel, you can't believe that you'll be happy with someone like her."

"What do you mean, Mom? Someone gorgeous, funny, smart, driven, and free thinking?" I scowled at her. "Or do you mean someone poor?"

"Well..." She trudged over to me and pursed her lips. "I think we need to continue this discussion when your father is here because it's obvious I'm not talking any sense into you."

"Goodbye, Mom," I called as she walked past me.

With the office door shut, I rubbed my forehead, frustrated. The intense relaxation I felt after sex was gone. Mom had seen to that. I slumped into my desk chair and stared blankly at the screen. It didn't matter to me that my parents didn't approve of Emily, though it would mean a lot to me if they at least gave her a shot.

I just hoped Mom didn't corner Emily in the outer office and lecture her. I didn't want that to be Emily's first impression of my family. They were great once you got to know them. It was just getting past their ridiculously high standards.

11

EMILY

For a lazy Saturday, my body acted like a rebellious child. I woke up before seven a.m. unable to fall back asleep, so while the rest of the world slept in, I scrolled my social media accounts, clearing notifications. The bed was too comfortable to get out of, but I knew if I didn't I'd be lying there for hours, losing half of my day. I tossed the covers back and set my phone on the nightstand, but it started vibrating, my mom's caller ID showing on the screen. I picked it up and answered, flinging myself back beneath the covers.

"Hey, Mom, what's up?"

"Well, good morning, dear. I didn't think you'd be awake yet. I thought maybe you'd be groggy when I called." I heard the sound of water running in the background on her end of the line. She was probably doing dishes after breakfast. She and Dad were always early risers.

"Well, I have to be up at five-thirty a.m. every morning for work now, so my body is adjusting and I can't seem to sleep in." I rubbed my eyes and waited for her to continue. It had been a few weeks since I talked to her. Not that I was avoiding home. I just got busy with work lately.

"Well, your sister called me. She's concerned about this man you're seeing."

My gut tightened. I closed my eyes and sighed deeply, hoping she didn't hear it. Why would Evelyn go straight to Mom and Dad and tell them about Daniel? It was none of her business who I dated or what I did in my personal life. Sometimes, I hated having an older sister who tattled on me for everything. I was old enough to make my own choices without parental consent.

"She said he's your boss? He's the head partner and CEO?"

"Mom, it's not a big deal." I had used the fact that Olivia was my direct boss to justify this relationship, but now that I reported directly to Daniel, it was probably a bit more unethical. "He's not that much older."

"Twelve years is a lot older, Emily." The tone of her voice told me either she or Evelyn had been researching him, which made me angry.

"Mom, I'm a grown woman. I can handle myself." I tossed the covers back and rolled out of bed, no longer comfortable. "I have been making my own decisions for five years now, and I live on my own, pay my own bills. Why can't you trust that I know what I'm doing?"

I strolled out to the kitchen and put a K-cup in my Keurig and turned it on. While the machine heated up, I grabbed a mug and placed it under the spout and got my cream and sweetener ready.

"Emily, you're so young. You haven't been around long enough to know when someone is manipulating you."

As she said the words, I gritted my teeth. Of course I knew when someone was manipulating me, like she was doing now. "I'm a big girl, Mom."

"He's probably using his authority as your boss to get you to do what he wants. When he tires of you, he'll fire you. Emily, your heart will be broken. He has probably done this to all of his assistants so far."

Mom's words sank in, but I refused to believe them. Yes, I'd had some of those exact fears, but I refused to believe Daniel was like that. "Mom, not every man on this planet is a jerk." The machine hissed, announcing the coffee was finished, so I mixed in the cream and sugar and slid the cream back into the fridge. Then I took my coffee and curled up on the couch.

"Emily, please. He's so much older than you. What if you get involved with this guy and find that you have nothing in common? What if you realize in your thirties that he's pushing fifty and going to bed before eight p.m. and you're wanting to go out? Or you want children but he's past his prime. You need someone your age."

"Mom, please. I think I can make my own decisions. I'm going to go. I have a lot to do today, okay? I'll call you next week."

Mom sounded upset, but at this point, I didn't care. We hung up, and I knew it wouldn't be the end of it. She'd have my dad on my case next, probably demanding I come home. But this was my life now. I had built my whole life around Chicago—new job, new apartment, the ability to support myself. There was no way I was going back to small-town Illinois and living under my parents' thumb.

I had half a mind to call Evelyn and tell her off right then, but this conversation would be better had in person. So I opened my calendar app on my phone. A notification popped up that I hadn't seen. I had been so busy I hadn't even opened my calendar in days. Five days, to be exact, because the health tracker that connected to my calendar app notified me that I had not confirmed the start of my period. I was supposed to start five days ago, and I hadn't started yet.

My heart dropped. I had unprotected sex with Daniel two times this month. Twice. I smacked my forehead and stewed for a second. How could I be so dumb? Part of me still wanted to tell Evelyn off, but now a bigger part of me felt really nervous. A pregnancy would complicate everything. My parents would really demand that I come home. Daniel—well, who knew what he'd say? We had only just decided that we were really going to make a go of this relationship. A baby would seriously mess that up. And my job—God, how would I support myself while taking weeks off after giving birth?

Panic set in, and I rushed to my bedroom and dressed. I didn't even take time to think. I put my shoes on, called an Uber, and raced down to the drug store to buy a pregnancy test. The woman at the counter scanned the test and took my debit card as if this were an everyday thing. People in the city probably went through this all the time, but in Monroe County, I'd have been the talk of the town. So, the anonymity of no one knowing me was nice, but I still had the same anxiety.

I rushed home just as fast, tearing the packaging on the test box in the wrong places so I ended up not having the directions. I had to Google what to do. I felt like an idiot because any other woman on this planet would have a sister or mother to help them. I considered calling Charlotte, but I was so embarrassed. She had warned me to protect myself and I hadn't. All I had thought about was how amazing Daniel was and how much I enjoyed spending time with him.

I almost started to cry as I held the little plastic stick in my stream of urine and waited for it to soak the cotton swab at the end. I couldn't watch it process. I laid it on the counter, washed my hands, and paced in the hallway outside the bathroom door. The idea of having kids was something I'd always thought about. I wanted kids. I wanted a huge family. I just thought it would be with someone I loved deeply after being married. Not this way.

But being a mother would mean the world to me. A little human to love me, to care for. I couldn't imagine the amount of work involved, but something in my gut secretly hoped that maybe I was pregnant. I felt like I was a yo-yo, being tossed up and down in emotions, exhilaration and sheer terror jerking me around.

I had so many doubts, so many fears. Most of them revolved around me and Daniel and our relationship. He would probably think I got pregnant on purpose and was using that to make him stay with me. It couldn't be farther from the truth, but I had watched two girls in my graduating class at college go through something similar. And for both of them, it was the end of the relationship. I pressed my hand to my forehead and uttered a prayer. I didn't want to think about things with Daniel ending. They'd only just started.

After checking the time on my phone and seeing that three minutes had passed, I pushed open the bathroom door and crept in. I had to check what the internet said again to determine the test results because the nerves had already made me forget. When I looked down at those tiny pink lines, I knew. My legs went weak, and I sat on the lid of the toilet. I picked up the test and stared at it.

"Pink..." I muttered, feeling a stupid grin cross my face.

My hand fluttered to my stomach. I expected to feel sick or terrified. I didn't. I stared at those pink lines and felt tears welling up. Happy tears.

"I'm pregnant." There was a little life growing inside me, one that Daniel and I created together. It was a living, breathing miracle and I was a part of it. Every fear that had just gone through my head for the past twenty minutes was gone, replaced with joy I couldn't express.

So what if it was happening earlier than I had planned, or in an unexpected way? I was going to be a mother, and I was instantly in love with the little boy or girl I was carrying. I wept for a solid ten minutes, clutching that test stick. I didn't know how I would tell anyone the news. Their reactions would be exactly as I feared, but I had to remain confident.

I wiped my eyes and tossed the test stick into the trash. First things first, I had to find out if Daniel even wanted children.

12

DANIEL

I glanced at my watch. It was nearly quitting time and my day had been nothing but meetings and calls for hours. I was exhausted and hungry. I strolled past Jill's new desk. She was happily typing away at her computer like always. "How's the new job? I hear you hired a new assistant for Olivia."

Her face lit up and she looked up at me. "Yes, sir. Jeffrey starts tomorrow with Olivia. He'll be a great fit for our team."

"Good, good. I'm glad things are working out for you." I tapped my fingers on the corner of her desk and moved on. I was glad to have Emily to myself now and that the subsequent shifts in personnel had been positive for everyone.

After stopping off at the men's room to relieve my bladder, I headed to my office. Emily was not at her desk as I expected her to be, but the door to my office was ajar. I always left it shut, so I knew Emily had to be in there working. It had become somewhat of a mutual workspace, shared because she did so much for me now that she needed more room to work.

As I walked in, I noticed the files and papers she had spread across the area rug. There were at least a dozen stacks of paper. She hovered there, placing copies of the sheets of paper in her hand onto the top of each pile.

"Collating? You know the copier will do that for you?"

"Yes, I know." She was brusque, leaning over the stacks without looking up. It wasn't like her to be abrupt with me, so I figured something was wrong.

I walked around her, careful not to step on any of her work, and pulled up a chair so I could sit and talk with her. She was busily sorting her paperwork, and I wondered why she hadn't just used the copier, but I didn't ask. I didn't want to upset her.

"How has your day been?"

She glanced up at me as I asked but refocused on her work. "Fine." I hadn't spoken to her much, but I didn't figure that was a reason for her to be this upset with me. We had a lot of days where communication was minimal and I found it challenging to carve out time during my workday to spend with her.

"Did I do something wrong?"

"No, you did nothing wrong. Okay?"

I sat and watched her collating all the files for at least twenty minutes. Her shoulders were tense, and her brow was furrowed. If I didn't know better, I would have thought she was upset with me, but she had told me that she wasn't upset with me, so that left me very confused. When she had all of her sheets distributed to the appropriate piles, she took each stack and stapled them. Then she stacked them all together.

As she pushed herself off the ground to stand, she gave me a great view of her ass. That skirt she wore fit her like a glove, and I couldn't resist saying, "Wow, your ass is incredible in that skirt. How about you come over here and sit on my lap and let me help you relax?"

"Look, D, I don't have time for this today." She dropped the papers on my desk. "The documents for your four o'clock tomorrow are here. You can check them out, but I did exactly what you said to do."

Emily turned to face me, and I noticed her sullen expression. It appeared there were tears in her eyes, though I didn't want to pry. "Are you okay?"

"I said, yes, I'm okay."

I stood and walked over to her. "You don't look okay." I reached for her, but she moved away, heading toward the couch. There was another stack of papers there that she picked up.

"Look, I just don't want to talk about it." She curled her hair around her ear and walked back to my desk, and this time, I didn't let her avoid my grasp.

"I care about you, Em. Look, something is wrong. Talk to me."

She looked down as if she was ashamed or afraid of talking to me, and I felt saddened that she would ever feel those emotions around me. Our relationship wasn't conventional, though, and I had been very busy and distracted. Even our lunches together had been crowded out by meetings for the past week.

"Look, can we talk?" she asked. She wrung her hands, and I nodded.

"Of course we can talk. Let's sit." I gestured toward the couch, and she walked with me and sat down. Her shoulders drooped. I could tell she'd been crying too. As close as I was, I saw the streaks through her makeup, long ago dried but still visible up close. "Tell me what's on your mind."

Emily sighed and said, "Well, I think if we're going to have a relationship, we need to make it official, you know?" She looked up at me with a hopeful expression. "I think just having lunch together when you're not busy and sex over your desk—it's not enough. I want more, D. I want to date you and have dinner. I want to see your house, and invite you to my apartment. I want to introduce you to my parents at some point, and I want to have sex in a bed. Not on a couch, or across a desk, or on a throw rug."

I wagged my eyebrows, remembering the sex over my desk. "That was pretty hot sex, though. You have to admit it."

My comment drew a smile to her lips, but it faded quickly and she looked down at her hands, still wringing together in her lap. I got the feeling there was something more bothering her, but I knew she'd open up in her good time.

"Yes, well, sex isn't enough for me. Okay? I need a future."

"Then let's start right now." I slapped my knees and stood up, and her eyes followed my motion.

"What do you mean, right now?"

"I mean, let's go have dinner. You and me. I'm starving. You've been working hard all day. I want to take my lady out for a delicious treat and enjoy her without the pressure of work weighing on us."

A smile curved her lips. "You mean that?" she asked, rising to stand with me.

"Yes, I mean that. Whatever you have going on with all this paperwork can wait until tomorrow. I'm taking you to Amelio's. It's this amazing pizza joint, but it's super classy. Picture the Godfather's bar, but not bar food. And they make the most amazing Moscow Mule ever."

"Uh, what's that?" Emily took my hand and followed me toward the door. I already had my phone in hand, sending a message to my driver to come around and pick me up.

"It's a Russian drink—beer and vodka with lime and something else... I can't remember. But you'll love it."

Emily blanched and shook her head. "No, thanks. I don't think I'm drinking."

The announcement surprised me. I hadn't really interacted with Emily outside of work, but I never took her for the purist type who didn't drink. I respected anyone who could get through life without a beer on occasion but preferred a drinking companion.

"You sure? My treat. I can get you a mojito, or a margarita. Whatever you want. It's dinner out. We're not on the clock. Might be fun to cut loose."

The more I coaxed her, the paler she got, and her hand cradled her stomach. "I'm not sure that's a good idea. I have to work in the morning, and what if I end up with a hangover or something? I think no drinking is best for me."

"Suit yourself. I hope you don't' mind if I have a drink?"

"Of course not. You can do as you please." Her smile returned as I placed my hand in the small of her back and guided her toward the elevator. Olivia watched us walk past, then Grace stopped to gawk. Jill looked up, eyes wide as I escorted my date to the elevator. Every staffer we strolled past got a good view of me and Emily walking far too close to be professional.

Emily tucked into my side, a timid mouse frightened by the beasts that devoured her with their eyes. "They're staring."

"Well, let them stare. In fact, we could give them something to talk about." I snickered, thinking about kissing her right there as we waited for the elevator doors to open, but she stepped away, pressing the call button a dozen times at least.

"I'd rather not be talked about right now."

As we passed Michael's office, I saw his death glare. He warned me to keep my distance, but I refused to be bullied by him. He stood and watched us walking, but he didn't follow us. For that I was thankful. While I would, at any cost, defend my choice to date Emily, I prayed it never came to an outright argument or disagreement in the office. And I didn't want to have that discussion in front of Emily, either. I'd hear about it tomorrow, but for tonight it was out of sight, out of mind.

Discouraged but not defeated, I kept my distance until we were in the car, at which point I pulled her against my body and kissed her hard. She seemed to hesitate for a moment but relaxed and let me deepen the kiss and grope her breast too. She moaned, but it sounded more like pain than pleasure, so I didn't do it again.

"This means a lot to me, that you are taking us seriously." Emily pulled away from me slightly, looking up into my eyes. Her hand remained resting on my chest.

"I told you I want to get to know you. We have some sort of chemistry going on that I've never had with anyone else, and I want to explore that."

As I was speaking, Emily's face grew bright with happiness. She looked past me out the window, and I turned to see what she was looking at. Cloud Gate had captured her attention, the giant bean-shaped artwork in the park, a huge tourist attraction. She stared and gawked for the thirty seconds it was in view, then sat back.

"Wow, there are so many things I haven't seen in this town."

"City," I corrected.

"Huh?"

"Chicago is a city, a very large one."

"Yeah, that's what I said. Anyway, you can take me to see all the sights someday. I know so little about it." She curled back into my side and rested her head on my shoulder.

Emily was a small-town girl, completely ignorant of city life. She probably saw more farms and tractors growing up than skyscrapers and taxis. It was something I'd have to get used to for sure, because I had zero interest in gallivanting around the city, showing her any sights. Chicago had lost the luster for me years ago. It was just a boring city to me now.

I wasn't about to give up on her, though. No matter how different we were, I was going to make it work.

13

EMILY

When I tried climbing out of the limo before the driver opened the door, Daniel scolded me. I knew he didn't mean to make me feel bad and he apologized at least three times before we even got to the door of the restaurant, but I burst out in tears anyway. My emotions were all over the place, and I hadn't been having very good days. I thought Evelyn was making it up when she told me how badly her hormones affected her in her first trimester with Jesse. Now I knew differently.

Daniel walked me to our table, and we ordered immediately. He knew the menu and had favorites, and I was so hungry I'd eat a horse, so I didn't balk at his suggestions. I ordered a diet soda and decided to be as content as I could. My heart weighed the idea of telling him about the baby tonight. It hadn't been that long at all, under two months, and I was really scared he would be upset, so I had a lot of pressure on my shoulders, but finally, I decided when the mood was right, I'd bring it up.

"Emily, you've been a little upset all day—all week, in fact. What's wrong? Are you not happy dating me?" He reached across the table and took my hand, and I let him hold it.

"No… Uh, I'm really happy dating you. I think we have something special. We have so much in common despite being so different in other ways. It's just..."

His face fell, brows drawn, eyes saddened. "What is it?"

"Well, first of all, you're my boss. And when we first started this thing, you weren't my direct boss. Olivia was. Now it's you. And I'm worried that people will talk about us. Before tonight, no one really knew. I mean, I'd heard gossip floating around the office, but no one came right out and asked me if something was going on. But now that they've seen us leaving together, and your arm was around me... They're going to talk."

I thought about how Evelyn's friends in high school would gossip about her behind her back, talking about the latest boy she'd been on a date with. At times, they spread nasty rumors about her and once even got a story going that she'd gotten pregnant and aborted the baby just to not lose her figure. I was scared that something similar may happen to me. Chicago might have treated me with anonymity when I bought that pregnancy test, but the office didn't have the population of the city. It was a group of tightly knit coworkers who knew a lot about each other.

"Look, if you're worried about that, I can lay down the law. People respect me, and I will force them to respect you too."

He squeezed my hand, but I wasn't reassured. Not knowing my stomach would begin growing soon and there would be no way to hide this secret from my peers. I had to push that thought away because it only churned up more emotion and I had to blink back tears.

"Okay, but what about the age difference?" My lip quivered as I spoke. "I mean, twelve years is a big difference. What do you think people will say about us when we go public for real? And what if you die before me? I can't marry someone who will die early and leave me a widow." That did it. Tears cascaded down my cheeks. The thought of my fifty-year-old husband dying when I was only thirty-seven and still had teenagers at home terrified me. Men died early all the time—heart attack, stroke, cancer. I shuddered at the thought.

"Okay, well I have no plans on leaving this earth until I'm in my nineties, so you can rest easy. Besides, we need to take one step at a time. Let's worry about whether we're able to date successfully before we jump into a marriage scenario." He chuckled, and I felt foolish for bringing up marriage on our first real date, but deep down, I knew if he knew about the baby, he'd either want marriage or he'd run for the hills.

"Okay, then... I want to be independent. I want to build my own career and pay my own way. I watched my mom having to do whatever my dad said because he was the sole breadwinner for so long. I want to have freedom to make choices."

"What makes you think you won't have freedom?" He nodded at the waiter who brought out our large pizza. We paused the conversation for a moment as he scooped a slice of pizza onto my plate then one onto his. I waited until he'd taken a bite before I continued.

"Well... so you make a lot of money. I barely make any. I'm thinking that's going to cause problems. You're not going to let me struggle and fail and learn how to do things. You'll jump in and save me, pay my way. I don't want a handout." I took a tiny bite of the pizza and realized how good it was. My stomach growled loudly. I hadn't had too much nausea yet, which was good, but I also had gone easy on eating anything acidic, and this sauce was so amazing I knew I'd overdo it.

"Alright, I promise not to bail you out or push my money on you. Okay?" Daniel sounded a bit perturbed by my worries, so I backed off. I ate my slice of pizza in silence and waited for him to speak. Maybe I had let my irrational fears carry me away.

"Why don't we talk about something else now? What about your family? What are they like?" He smiled and took another bite of pizza. This was a topic I wanted to avoid entirely, but he had brought it up, so there was no getting out of it.

"Well, my parents are entrepreneurs, like I told you. They are very family oriented and overprotective, one of the reasons I came here. Evelyn is sort of controlling like Mom, though she can go days without even talking to me, which is nice. Sometimes, I need a break." I wiped my mouth and sipped my soda.

"Interesting... So where do you see yourself in five or ten years?"

"I want to maybe move out of the city. Not necessarily back to Monroe County, but not Chicago. It's big and nice, but I'm here for the opportunity. I hope maybe I'll have a few kids, a strong career... You know, the American dream."

Daniel eyed me, and I watched his shoulders fall a bit as he scooped another slice of pizza onto his plate.

"What about you? Where do you see yourself in ten years?" I helped myself to another slice, but I warned myself not to eat too much more than that. I really was worried that morning sickness would hit at the worst possible time. I did not want to end up vomiting pizza in the restaurant's bathroom.

"Well, I see myself running my established practice here in Chicago. I want to open branches in New York and LA. I've always been a huge fan of the city and don't really have a plan to leave."

My heart sank a little at his future plans. While I loved the city and had chosen to move here, I knew it was a stepping stone toward my future, similar to how I felt about taking the job at the firm. My plans didn't involve living in a city long term. I noticed he also hadn't mentioned anything about having a family, so despite my discouragement over his hoped-for dwelling location, I pushed on.

"And a family? I think two or three kids, maybe. I loved having a sister to grow up with, though at times, we fought. I just couldn't imagine growing up with no siblings, though. My friend Amanda was an only child, and she hated it. She told me how her parents were so micromanaging and overbearing because they had no other children to pay attention to." I chuckled as I remembered the story, but Daniel shrugged.

"Not sure. I've never really seen myself as a family man, per se. I mostly focus on my career and my clients. It takes a lot of work to run a company by yourself, and I haven't even had time to date, let alone have kids." He chomped on his pizza, and my heart plunged to the depths of the ocean.

I tried not to let the emotion overwhelm me, but I felt tears coming again. "Uh, I have to use the restroom." I forced a smile. "I'll be right back, okay?"

"Sure." Daniel smiled at me and took another bite of food, and I slipped away. The tears streamed down my cheeks before I got myself locked into a stall, and I sat there with my shoulders heaving with sobs.

I was so emotional over the stupidest things lately, but this wasn't a stupid thing. If Daniel didn't want to be a father, I was in huge trouble. My mind swirled with thoughts I couldn't express. I was already pregnant. It wasn't like we were thinking of planning a family together. He didn't know anything about the baby, and all I could think was how angry he would be when he found out. I'd ruined the plans for his future. I pictured a bleak existence where I struggled to make ends meet as a single mother while he lived his best life in the big city.

"Are you okay?" a soft voice asked me along with a knock on the stall door. I sat on the toilet but hadn't even pulled my pants down, so I opened it up and saw a waitress there with compassion in her eyes.

"I'm pregnant, and my boyfriend just told me he didn't see himself having a family." I sobbed louder. It felt good to get it off my chest.

"Oh, honey." She crouched in front of me. "Listen, you can do this. It's not the end of the world. Okay? I'm a single mom and I'm killing it. There are so many opportunities in Chicago." She rested her hand on my knee, but her words were not so comforting. It was further proof that I'd made a mistake.

"Thank you." I grabbed some toilet paper and blew my nose. "I think I should just go back to the table. I appreciate your listening."

"Sure, no problem, hun."

I took a few minutes to wash my face and reapply my mascara before heading back to the table. Daniel wasn't there, so I sat alone and ate another slice of pizza I'd probably regret later on. When he returned, presumably from the bathroom or from paying the check, he looked concerned.

"Are you okay, Emily? I've been asking what's wrong all day and you just aren't talking to me. It's clearly more than just my being your boss or what coworkers will say."

"I… Uh, I'm sorry Daniel. I got a call from my mom this week and it just really upset me. Okay? It's nothing you need to worry about."

"You've been crying again. I worry about that." He reached for my face and cupped my cheek. I was comforted by his gesture, but my heart was still really sad.

"I'm okay, really."

"Well, you're down, and I don't want to take you home to sit alone while you're down. You can come to my place. I'll show you around, and we can have a drink or just sit on the patio and talk."

"Work tomorrow… How will I be ready? I have no clothes at your house." I hesitated. The way he had pressured me to drink earlier made me very uncomfortable. I liked a glass of wine or spirits as much as anyone else, but not while pregnant. I loved this little life inside me more than life itself. There was no way I was caving to that peer pressure, and he would wonder why. "Maybe tonight isn't a good night."

"Nonsense. It's a perfect night. I'll have the driver bring you home to change before work, and it will be fine."

His insistence that he protect and watch over me was sweet. I nodded. "Okay, I'll go." I rose with him as he dropped a few bills on the table as a tip. If he pressured me to drink, I'd just have to tell him. Besides, his home was a much better place to have that argument than a restaurant. It was inevitable, anyway…

14

DANIEL

I let Emily in, waving the maid off at the door. She gawked upward at the large crystal chandelier hanging in the foyer, her mouth hanging open. At first I chuckled at her reaction, the way she ran her fingers along the picture frames of the French paintings hanging on the wall, but then doubt began to creep in as I remembered my mom's accusations against Emily's character. I observed her for a moment, pondering.

"God, Dan, these things are worth millions of dollars." She rushed over to a small stand with a vase sitting on it. It was a one-of-a-kind Émille Gallé straight out of Paris that I had imported to match the paintings. She started to pick it up, but I interrupted, taking it from her hands carefully.

"Some things are better left untouched."

Her eyes went wide. "It's expensive?"

"Everything in this house is expensive." I set the vase back on the stand and hooked my arm around her waist. "Let's go see about that drink."

Emily stiffened when I mentioned a drink, which she previously refused, but I guided her toward my den anyway. She glanced over her shoulder at the vase and walked with me as I flipped on lights along the way.

"I'd show you around the entire place, but the staff is probably mostly asleep by now. We can just entertain ourselves for a while." I smirked at her, hoping she understood my meaning. The way her cheeks flushed indicated she understood.

"You have very expensive taste."

"I do, but it's because I want for nothing. I don't work because I have to. I work because I enjoy working. I love doing my job." I flicked on the light in my den and let her in. She gasped at the wall of books, shelves stretching floor to twelve-foot ceiling. My collection of classics and certain first editions were organized in order of monetary value, with the most expensive to replace being safely stored in sealed plastic on the top shelf. Though my first edition *Gatsby* was front and center on a shelf just below eye height. Emily was immediately drawn to it, touching the glass enclosure gently. The exact reason I had that particular one in a case. Everyone loved to touch it, and since Emily was a book lover, I didn't mind fingerprints on the glass.

"You have a *Gatsby*?" Her eyes wide, she looked back at me, a half-grin curling her lips.

"I do, but you can't touch it. Books that old have to be stored in very careful conditions so they don't get damaged."

"Of course they do." She leaned in and cocked her head, presumably so she could read the spine. "I've never seen a first edition. How much was it?"

There it was again, the mention of something's price. Maybe it was because we were so different, or maybe it was because I had only really entertained women of a much wealthier status, but Emily seemed both alluring and alarming in the same breath. Mother could very well have been right about her being a gold digger, but I didn't want to believe it, so I chose to believe the former. She wasn't used to being surrounded by such pricey things.

I poured myself a glass of bourbon and downed it in one swallow, not even bothering to ask her if she wanted a drink. After her previous reactions, I knew what her answer would be. "Well, the copy

I have has a smudge on page one hundred twenty-three, but I paid two hundred fifty thousand for it." I set the glass on the liquor cabinet and joined her by the books. "You are a fan?"

"You know I love reading. Do you have Dumas?" She smiled at me, clinging to my lapels.

"I do. My first edition *Monte Cristo* is valued at eighty-two thousand. The *Musketeers* that I have is worth twenty-five. They're in great shape, and also both sealed in plastic and on the top shelf where oily fingers can't destroy them." I leaned down and kissed her. "All this talk about my books is tiring. I think maybe we should just relax a bit."

"You said you loved reading, but I had no clue you had such a great collection." Emily wrapped her arms around my neck. "Thank you for showing me."

She seemed to be feeling better. I wrapped my arms around her waist and leaned down to kiss her, a soft, savory kiss this time, parting her lips and nipping at her tongue.

"I'd like to show you something else." I pulled her hard against my body, crushing her breasts between us. "And it's upstairs in my bedroom."

"The bedroom?" she joked, pulling my mouth toward hers again.

"No. If I have it my way, the only thing you'll be seeing are stars." I continued kissing her as I backed her toward the door. She seemed to drag her feet a little, so I lifted her up, forcing her legs around my hips. When I did, her body loosened up, allowing me to be in control. I carried her up the stairs to my dimly lit room and dropped her on the bed. I had her clothes off her before she could protest, and mine fell into the same pile.

She lay on the bed quivering, her eyes dilated with lust and desire, her lips parted as she panted. Her skin was smooth and soft. I ran my hand over her and felt every ridge, bump, and crevice, becoming familiar with her body at last. "D..." she panted as my palm slid over her breast, and I squeezed it. I could smell her shampoo as I nuzzled her neck. Though it was sweet and floral, it carried with it the subtle musk of her arousal.

The sun had just set, casting a beautiful golden hue on the room. I felt her soft breath on my cheek as I moved closer to her, my finger-tips trailing over her creamy skin as I explored her curves. She shiv-ered beneath my touch, her lips parting in anticipation of my kiss. I leaned in and kissed her hard, taking her breath away.

The kiss was intense, sending a surge of warmth through my veins. The room seemed to spin, and a thousand stars danced around us. We were wrapped in an aura that only we could feel, and I wanted to stay in this moment forever.

"God, you're so beautiful." I ground my hips against her pelvis, feeling my cock slide through her juices. Her moans of enjoyment echoed through the room, the walls vibrating with sound.

The way she rose up to meet me as my body rubbed against her, pushing my fingers into her was erotic. Dangerous. I looked down at her, her eyes closed and her mouth slightly agape. Her cheeks were flushed and she was breathing heavily. She was completely at my mercy, and I reveled in the power it gave me.

I ran my hands slowly over her body, exploring her curves with renewed fascination. She shivered as my fingers trailed down her arms and across her stomach. When I reached her thighs, she parted them eagerly in anticipation.

Her pussy dripped with nectar, arousal slicking her soft folds. I pressed my fingers into it, feeling her tense and jolt with pleasure. She moaned and writhed beneath me, and I felt my own body respond in kind.

I moved my fingers in a slow, circular motion, going deeper and deeper until her whole body was quivering and trembling. My other hand caressed her breasts and neck as I continued to tantalize her.

Her breathing became more and more erratic, and I knew that she was close. I increased the pressure and speed of my fingers, pushing her closer and closer to the edge. Finally, with one final thrust, she let out a shuddering cry as her orgasm took her over the edge.

"Ahh," she moaned, convulsing beneath me.

"Good girl," I growled into her ear, biting her earlobe and sucking on it. She sank her teeth into my shoulder and spasmed, clawing at my back. The orgasm lasted several minutes. Each time it waned, swelling again with renewed vigor on the part of my fingers massaging her. And when she calmed, I forced her legs farther apart.

She let out a tiny gasp as I slid into her, our bodies folding together in perfect harmony. I could feel her breath on my skin as I moved, each motion a moment of exquisite pleasure and anticipation. My cock dived into her, plunging into her abyss over and over. Her pussy clenched around me, milking me. I groaned as the pleasure built inside me to an unbearable intensity.

My hands caressed her curves as I moved, my mouth exploring her neck and her shoulders. Her breath came in short gasps as her orgasm neared, and I felt my own rising within me.

Finally, I could no longer contain myself and my climax filled her body. I let out a deep, guttural cry as my body pulsed and released, completely drained yet still connected to her in an intimate embrace. We lay there afterwards, panting, our skin slick with sweat and our hearts pounding. It was the closest we had ever been, the most alive either of us had ever felt. It was a moment of perfect bliss, where nothing else mattered.

And when we were finally still, I held her close, feeling her heart beating against mine. We lay there, entwined in one another, our breathing slowly returning to normal, the night around us fading away. For that moment, we were connected in a way that transcended words, a communion of souls I had never known before.

It felt like a dream, one that I never wanted to end. But dreams aren't always reality, and when she spoke, I was brought back to the present.

"D, do you really think we're compatible? That we can make this work?" Emily curled into my chest, and I held her. She kissed my skin, and I pressed my lips to her forehead.

"I think we can do whatever we put our minds to. I think if you want to be with me and I want to be with you, then nothing in the world will stop us. We just have to work at it."

She sighed contentedly, and I pulled the covers up over us. "I'm sorry if something I said at dinner upset you. I noticed you were crying when you came back from the bathroom, and the last thing I want to do is hurt you. Emily, if you're not okay with this, please tell me. We will work something out. I can assign you as assistant to Olivia again, or Michael. It will make things less stressful for you at work. We will just get less time together."

I lay there waiting for a response, but one didn't come. I pulled away slightly and saw her eyes shut and heard soft snores. She looked like an angel wrapped in cotton, sleeping on my pillow. How could someone so perfect cause so much doubt? My mother had no clue what she was talking about, and I was an idiot for doubting Emily. She was so wonderful, so kind. Granted, she was a bit naïve when it came to certain aspects of life, but I found that part of her sweet and innocent. I never wanted to change that about her.

"I think I'm really falling for you, Em." I kissed her forehead again and pulled her into my chest.

"Mmm, can you cover me? I'm cold," she mumbled, but I knew she was talking in her sleep. I held her tightly to keep her warm. I'd never let her go again if I had my way, but we would wake tomorrow and life would thrust itself up on us. So for now, I enjoyed her as she was —mine.

15

EMILY

I sat at my desk waiting for the clock to tick over to three o'clock. Daniel asked me to bring in the packets of information I'd put together last week at that time, and I felt nervous. As his assistant, part of my job required that I sometimes interact with the other partners, and after overhearing Grace tell Daniel that inner-office dating was unethical, I tried to avoid any interaction with her. Today, it would be unavoidable.

I tapped my fingers nervously as Jill approached. She noticed my tapping and stopped by my desk and leaned on it. "Everything okay?" she asked, folding her arms over her chest. She was a sweet woman, always ready to help me learn anything I didn't already know, since she had been in this position before me. I shrugged.

"I'm okay. Just a bit nervous today. I have to interrupt the partners during their meeting at three. Mr. Jacobs requested for me to bring these files. They just intimidate me is all." I picked at my fingernails and tried not to get too worked up. My emotions were already running rampant, making me cry at the drop of a hat.

"Oh, don't let them get to you. You're doing fine. If you have Mr. Jacobs's approval, that's all you need. You just march right in there like you own the place, and you'll see that they respect you." Jill patted my hand and stood. "Besides, they like you. I'm sure of it. Benjamin told me the other day that Daniel is far more organized and on top of things. I think you were exactly what he needed. You seem to be whipping him into shape in ways I never could. Good job."

I forced a smile and glanced up at the clock as she walked away. Now only minutes until I had to take the paperwork in, I took a deep, cleansing breath to calm myself. Jill was right. If Daniel approved of me, it really didn't matter if they liked me or not. I didn't report to them, and I didn't have to even talk to them throughout my workday. I stood and collected my papers and strolled over to the office door. As soon as the clock ticked over, I opened the door and strutted in with confidence.

"Ah, perfect timing." Daniel stood and straightened his tie. He always stood when I entered the room. I sort of liked it.

"Here you go, Mr. Jacobs, the files you requested." I handed him the papers, but I noticed the partners were staring at me. If I hadn't known better, I'd have thought maybe I had a stain on my shirt or a booger or something. I swallowed away the nerves and pointed at the stack. "I made copies for everyone, and here you'll see that the client's budget is highlighted as you requested. Is there anything else?"

"I think that's all. Thank you, Emily." He smiled at me, and I turned to go when Benjamin chimed in.

"Actually, we were just having a little debate, Emily. Mind settling it for us?" He grinned and looked at Michael, who looked irritated that I was even in the room with him. He was the one who made me the most nervous.

"Uh…" I glanced around. Olivia looked down at her cell. Grace scowled at Daniel, and I was left feeling jittery, wishing I could run out. "Sure?"

"Alright, so we want to know which is the most famous landmark. The bean, or Wrigley." He looked at Michael again, smirking. "Mike over here thinks it's the bean, but I know it's Wrigley."

I licked my lips and felt my throat constricting. I'd heard of Wrigley Field before but had no clue what he meant by the bean. Maybe that was the point. He was trying to prove that everyone had heard of baseball stadiums, but some other lesser landmark was insignificant. I faltered, finding my hands searching for each other so I could pick my nails.

"Well? Which is it?" Michael insisted, raising an eyebrow.

"I'm sorry, sir. I don't think I know what the bean is. Maybe it goes by another name?" I felt foolish. I knew nothing about the city. I hadn't even taken time to sightsee or explore. Since I moved here, I had been working all the time. I couldn't even look at Daniel. I felt like I was embarrassing him too, considering people had seen us leaving together, so they likely assumed we were dating.

"The bean?" Michael's eyebrows rose and drew together in the middle. "You've never heard of the bean? Cloud gate? Millennium Park?" He laughed, and I looked down at my feet, unable to look at the others' faces.

"Come on, guys. She's new to town." Daniel sticking up for me was the last thing I needed. It was pity. I hated pity. Like the time one of Evelyn's ex boyfriends wanted to date me after breaking up with her because he felt sorry for my not having anyone interested in me. It was degrading.

"Look, Wrigley it is." Benjamin was doing it too, trying to redirect the conversation away from my humiliation.

"No, it's sort of funny, though," Michael said. "The bean is so huge, who could miss it? A giant, silver, bean-shaped piece of art."

As he described what it was, I instantly remembered the night Daniel drove me across town for dinner and I saw the massive silver blob. I had no clue what it was called. I'd never heard of it before coming to Chicago, though, so Benjamin's point stood. Everyone had heard of Wrigley field, but not everyone had heard of the bean.

"We need to get back to business," Daniel said, dropping the papers on the table in front of himself. "Emily, come with me." He moved toward the door, and I followed behind him, shuffling my feet. I felt the eyes of everyone in the room on me, like I was the leper in the camp being ushered out of town before I infected anyone else. When the door was shut behind us, I felt my eyes welling up.

"I'm so sorry. I am humiliated." I pinched the bridge of my nose to stop the tears from coming.

He took me by the arms, talking softly to me. "Emily, are you okay? Those guys are rude sometimes. I'm sorry."

"You know, I don't know. It's quitting time in like an hour. Can I just go home? I don't want to cry in front of these people." I swiped at my rebellious eyes and sniffled.

"Sure, you can. I'll call you later, okay? If you need anything, you call me." Without any shame, Daniel leaned in and kissed my forehead. "Be safe."

I stood there for a moment after he'd let himself back into the conference room, then relaxed my shoulders, got my purse from my desk, and headed for the elevator. I made my way to the subway and found a spot to sit, deciding I needed to talk to someone about how I felt, so I called Charlotte, who answered on the first ring.

"Hey, Em, what's up?"

I blinked hard, keeping the tears away, and cleared my throat to ensure my voice didn't quaver as I spoke. "Well, I'm humiliated. Work was literally just a shit show, and I wanted to cry."

"Oh, gosh, what happened? You broke up with Dan?" Her first question made me bristle, the fact that she thought that made me sad, probably because I feared it was how things would end, anyway.

"Uh, no, but I'm a little worried about things with him too. That's a different story, though." I chewed my nail as I stared out the window. The subway pulled out of the station, moving slowly. I watched out the window as pedestrians on the platform waited on the next train while we zipped away.

"So tell me what happened," Charlotte said.

"I mean, it was nothing major, and I guess the situation is actually more connected to whether Daniel and I will make it or not than I realized. Char, I don't think we are similar enough. Dan likes the city. I want to move away from here eventually. He is so bold and outgoing, and I'm really shy. He's got all this power, his entire career built. I'm just starting out. I have nothing. He's rich. I'm living off ramen and using a laundromat." My eyes burned with unshed tears.

"Gosh, is that all?"

"No, I mean… Well, he doesn't see himself being a father. I want kids, a lot of them. You know how much that means to me." Hearing it all out loud, it was finally sinking in. We weren't even compatible. We came from different worlds. "Why am I even dating him? Evelyn was right. This is a disaster." I let the tears fall freely.

"No, stop that. Em, you're the Yin to his Yang, the peanut butter to his jelly. You don't eat a ketchup sandwich and put ketchup on it. You need the meat!" Charlotte chuckled. "You're seeing it all wrong. Opposites attract for a reason. You even him out. What makes you think his power won't leave room for you to have your own? Or that his money has to override anything you do? You can be a little bit of country to tone down his city-boy attitude."

I appreciated her humorous attempt to make me feel better, but I'd already decided my fate. I was too different from him, mostly because I was pregnant and I knew he didn't want kids. Or at least that's what he'd said. He didn't see himself as a father. That difference was one that would definitely divide us. I couldn't see us coming back from this when I told him I was pregnant.

"Hey, Char, I really appreciate your talking with me, but I'm just not feeling good anymore. I think I'm going to nap the rest of the ride home."

"Yeah, okay. Well, I'll be here all night. I have no plans." She sounded defeated, and I hated making her feel like that. She usually had a knack for helping me, but today was just not that sort of day.

"I'll call you later, maybe."

"Alright, bye." Char hung up, and I put my phone away. I had to figure out how to tell Daniel I was pregnant with his kid. I just knew he was going to be upset about it, and for that reason, I decided to wait. I cried about everything already. When I told him, I wanted to feel level-headed, not emotional.

I just didn't know how long it would be before my emotions settled down.

16

DANIEL

The mood was tense when I walked back into the office. Michael glared at me as I strolled back to my spot at the head of the table. I could tell they had been talking about me while I was out, and I was certain the kiss I gave Emily hadn't helped. Olivia stared at the paper in front of her. As a junior partner, she had zero say in higher level decisions, and honestly, none of them had a right to tell me how to live my personal life.

"What?" I snapped, sitting down. I tucked my tie into my jacket and rolled the chair closer to the table. Grace wasn't shy about the nasty look she was giving me, and Benjamin seemed amused by the way Michael and Grace were acting.

"What? You really have to ask that question?" Michael's nostrils flared as he leaned forward and pushed the papers away from himself. "Dan, we talked about this. You are treading on thin ice. You understand how very different you and Emily are? How just one wrong comment could send her running toward litigation?"

"What are you talking about? We're in a relationship we both want." I tried to fight my outrage, but it was growing by the second. "I told you to stay out of my personal life."

"Sir, with all due respect, your personal life will affect your job."

Grace cleared her throat nervously. At least she had the decency to be anxious about the way she spoke to me, unlike Michael. He'd been with me so long, he didn't even hesitate to say what was on his mind, which is why when Emily and I did something in my office, I had started having her lock the door, afraid he'd walk right in at any moment.

"My personal life is entirely separate from my ability to perform as a lawyer. If I were dating someone outside this office, it would be the same."

"Sir, if Emily—"

"If Emily does what, Grace? If she decides she wants my money? I'll give it to her. If she decides she wants my power? Hers. You can't put a price on love." Once the word was out of my mouth, there was no taking it back. Michael's eyebrows rose and so did he, leaning over the table menacingly.

"You can't think you love her. This is just some passing fancy. She's a baby, Daniel. A child. You are a grown man." He snorted out a laugh and shook his head. "You were in love with Keri too, and look how that turned out."

Just the mention of her name enraged me. I was on my feet ready to deck him instantly, and Ben had to hold me back. "Whoa, Dan… Take it easy." Ben pressed his hand in my chest, and I gritted my jaw.

"You know damn well that Keri was just using me. She ruined me. She could have bankrupted me." I pointed my finger at him as I shouted, knowing the outer office could both hear and see me.

"Exactly! I warned you about her. And I'm warning you about Emily too. You don't even see it. She's using you, manipulating you and twisting everything around here. One day, you're going to get slapped with a lawsuit for sexual harassment, and your name will be plastered on every single television screen in America. You'll be no better than Cosby or Clinton." Michael collected his papers and tapped them on the desk.

Olivia looked up at me, lip trembling, and I stared right at her. "What do you think, Olivia? You think that's what Emily is like? Is she just weaseling her way into my heart to sue me and take me for all I'm worth?" It was a rhetorical question, but she responded.

"No, sir, I don't think so, but none of us really believed Keri was capable of what she did, either." She shook as she spoke, still quite intimidated by being with the partners. I started toward Michael again, but Ben spoke softly in my ear.

"Let him go, Boss. He's got to blow steam." His hand pressed into my chest more firmly, and I ran a hand through my hair in frustration.

"When it happens, don't expect the firm to bail you out this time." Michael stormed off, letting the door slam behind him as he left.

"I'm afraid I agree with Mike, Daniel. If you continue down this path, you're going to regret it. While I can't condone Michael's behavior here today, I also can't stand behind your relationship with an employee. In today's climate with the "me too" movement, you're asking for trouble. He's right. The tabloids and news media would eat this up, a sexual harassment nightmare. We'd lose reputation and some very conservative clients." Grace pushed her chair away from the table, picked up her papers, and stood. "I'm sorry, sir." She walked out a bit more calmly than Michael had, and Ben let go of me.

"What the hell am I supposed to do?" I pinched the bridge of my nose and rubbed my face.

"I think love is love, and if you're really in a committed relationship with her, then you make it work and those guys will get over it. What is love without a little conflict? And besides, you're the head partner. What can they do?" Benjamin patted my shoulder.

"Thanks for not letting me do something stupid, Ben." I sighed and let the tension fall off my shoulders.

"Of course. Now just go home or something. Give yourself some time to cool off too." Ben left, and Olivia got up sheepishly, collected her paperwork and his, and wiggled her fingers in a goodbye before following him out of the conference room.

I didn't understand why they were so upset about my relationship. I could see they were concerned, especially Michael after what Keri had done and the way the firm had to stand behind me, but Emily was different, and they refused to get to know her.

The chair behind me became my refuge for the next forty minutes while I stewed over Michael's attitude. He'd been against this from the beginning with the same concerns about Emily, but if she was going to file suit against us, she'd have done it ages ago. We were in a good place, though I knew she'd been emotional lately, but I honestly felt like things were going well for us. When she voiced her concerns about wanting more than just "office sex", as she'd called it, I took it seriously.

I reached for my phone, dialing her number. I wanted to see if she would join me at my house tonight for dinner. After a frustrating afternoon, I didn't really want to dine alone, and I could think of no better company than her. Only the line rang straight through to voicemail. I didn't leave a message. If she was still embarrassed or upset by the way Michael had treated her, I knew she probably needed space.

So I sent a message to my driver to pick me up and took my paper-work back to my desk where I collected my wallet and keys. Walking out through the outer office felt like playing Russian roulette, not knowing if I was going to run into Michael or not, but he and Grace were speaking in hushed tones in her office as I passed. It was better that way. I knew if he started shit again, I'd just punch him and regret it. Olivia was already gone, and Ben was nowhere in sight, so I rode the elevator to the ground floor with a janitor and his mop bucket.

When my driver finally pulled into my drive, I noticed my parents' car in the driveway. It was the last thing I expected, to have surprise visitors, but there was no pretending I wasn't home or hadn't seen it. Dad stood on the front stoop smoking a cigar. He never smoked in the house because Mom wouldn't allow it. He'd seen me pull up. I waited until the driver opened the door for me and slowly climbed out. I just wanted to relax, not have more lectures about Emily and her status or value, or whether I should be with her.

My shoulders squared, I strolled up to the front door and nodded at Dad as I did. He puffed out some smoke and dropped his cigar, stamping it out on the cement. He kicked the half-burnt butt into the landscaping and turned to follow me as I reached for the door.

"Well, son, your mother and I wanted to chat with you. Your maid let us in. I hope you don't mind."

"Yeah..." I muttered. What else could I even say? I could tell by the tone of his voice that he intended to grill me, and it hardened the edge I'd had since about three-fifteen this afternoon.

"Oh, Daniel," Mom squawked when I walked into the den, "you've had that woman to your house?"

Confused, I paused just inside the door, and Dad bumped into my back. I glanced around the room, finding my maid standing by my liquor cabinet. Her cheeks were red and her head was down. Leave it to Mom to badger my staff into divulging things they should otherwise never speak of.

"Yes, I have," I said, glaring at the maid. "Remind me to find more faithful staff."

Mom scoffed and waved her hand, and the maid curtsied and said, "I'm sorry, sir." She scurried out of the room after handing me a glass of scotch she poured for me. She probably knew I'd need it for this. I downed it in two swallows and set it on the coffee table before pacing in front of the bookshelves.

"Daniel, your mother and I are quite concerned. We know you're looking for someone to spend your life with, but you need to find someone who fits you." Dad spoke as if he had someone in mind. I heard him snapping his fingers and looked up, turning to see him waving someone in the room. She was gorgeous—tall, blonde, curvy —but not Emily. "This is Bethany. She is a fourth-year law student at Harvard. She's the daughter of one of my colleagues, comes from a wealthy family. She's closer to your age, Dan. She's almost thirty, and yes, she went back to college to get her law degree, but that was after earning her Ph.D."

My chest tightened. As much as I wanted to scream at him how stupid he was, I didn't want to drag this poor woman into my family drama. I walked over to her and extended my hand. "Hello, Bethany, it's very nice to meet you."

"Same, Daniel. Our fathers have been friends for a while, so I've heard about you over the years. When your father offered to introduce me to you, I was flattered." She blushed as she retracted her hand and clutched her black purse in front of herself.

"If you will excuse us for a moment, I think I have something I need to discuss with my parents alone. It was really nice meeting you." I gestured toward the door, and she nodded, looking disappointed. As soon as she was out the door, I let it rip.

"What sort of maleficent bullshit are you trying to pull!" I glanced between Mom and Dad. Irate didn't begin to explain how I felt. "I am in a relationship. You are not Cupid. You can't just bring other women into my home and announce them as if you've found a match made in heaven."

"I'm sure once you calm down, you'll see that Bethany is a far better match for your personality, your financial status, even your education." Mom stood and hooked her purse over her arm and sauntered toward me. "She's even far prettier than that bimbo at work."

"Emily is not a bimbo!"

"Oh, Danny, you know we only want what's best for you." Mom patted my cheek and smiled at me. I politely took her by the wrist and removed her hand from my cheek.

"You don't want what's best for me. You want what's best for you. You think my dating someone you perceive as beneath you is bad optics. Well guess what? I'm dating her, and we're an item now."

"You can't be serious," Dad interjected. "That's ludicrous."

"Get out of my house." I pointed at the door, glaring at both of them. "Now. Get out. I'm done with this conversation. Thank Bethany for coming. I'm not interested."

I turned my back on them, picking up my glass on the way to my liquor cabinet, and heard the door shut as I poured a drink. God, I wished Emily were there for me to prove to them how amazing she was.

I drank the glass and poured another, then slumped onto the sofa in my den. They were wrong. All of them were. I would never jeopardize my job or my future if I thought Emily was out to play me. I would fight tooth and nail to prove her worth and my love for her because I loved her. Even if she had responded to my advances with ulterior motives, I knew she had a pure heart now. There was no way she was playing me.

I sipped my whiskey and closed my eyes, laying my head back. But as I took another sip, memories of Emily flooded my mind. Memories of her laughter, her touch, her soft curves pressed up against me. I felt my body stir with desire, and I knew that I needed her. I needed her more than anything else in the world.

I wasn't giving up, and I wasn't letting anything get in my way.

17

EMILY

I slogged into my apartment, dripping wet from the three-block walk from the subway station in the rain. My shoes squished water out with each step, leaving puddles along the way. I felt frustrated that I hadn't remembered my umbrella, but I'd been so preoccupied with Daniel and worrying about how to tell him I was pregnant that I hadn't even checked the weather. There was no one to blame but myself.

I peeled my suit jacket off, dropping it on the door mat next to my shoes, then set my purse down. It, too, dripped from the shower it had gotten, but the contents inside were safe, protected by the leather from which it was made. I was cold, shivering, and hungry, but I needed to warm up first. After the long day of work, and the emotional weight of being pregnant, I knew I needed some alone time to unwind and relax. I decided that a hot shower would do the trick.

I undressed quickly, trying to ignore the chill in the air, and stepped into the shower. My wet clothes lay on the floor in a puddle I'd have to clean up later. Immediately, I felt the hot water cascading down my body, like sweet relief after a long day. I put my head under the water and began to wash my hair. The sound of rushing water was loud. I closed my eyes, letting the warmth ease my worries and wash away my weariness.

I let the shower run, my thoughts racing as I processed the events of the day and pondered the changes coming into my life. I felt the warmth of the water and the steam around me, and for a moment, I was lost in my own world.

Eventually, I opened my eyes and stepped out of the shower. I felt a wave of comfort, the steam still lingering around me like a hug. As I was drying off, I caught a glimpse of myself in the mirror. Soon, my body would change in miraculous ways, but I'd be unable to hide it. That made my gut clench as I remembered that I still had to tell Daniel. I got dressed, now feeling warm, at least.

I was famished. As I walked out to the kitchen, my stomach grumbled unpleasantly. I had been so preoccupied with my worries about being pregnant that I had forgotten to eat all day. Now, my body was demanding sustenance.

I walked to the kitchen and opened the refrigerator door. Inside, a half-empty bottle of wine glinted in the dim light, beckoning me. I stared at it for a moment and then closed the door firmly. As much as I wanted to drown my troubles in a glass of wine, I knew that I had to be responsible and abstain while pregnant. And the fridge was nearly bare. It had been weeks since I grocery shopped, and the lack of lettuce, milk, and eggs was a clear sign that I was out of fresh things to eat.

The smell of my greasy leftover Chinese food was a pungent reminder of how long I'd gone without a home-cooked meal. I could already feel the healthy dinner I'd prepare in my head. My mouth watered at the prospect of a home-cooked meal with a glass of red wine, everything perfect and pure, but I managed to shut the fridge and move away.

I rummaged through the cupboards instead, eventually coming up with a few items to prepare a rudimentary meal. A handful of pitted olives, some stale crackers, a tomato, a hunk of cheese, and a jar of pickles were all I could find.

I laid out my ingredients on the counter and worked quickly to assemble a meal. Fried olives and cheese with tomato slices, served with crackers and pickles. It wasn't gourmet, but it would do.

As I ate, I kept thinking about what I would do if Daniel didn't want to be a father. Could I support the baby financially? I was full of worries, and no matter how much I ate, the gnawing feeling in my stomach wouldn't go away. It was a cancer eating away at my mental stability. The food only served to numb the physical pain of hunger but did nothing to sate the beast that wanted to prey on my heart.

When I finished the meager meal, I tossed the leftovers out, including the leftover Chinese, and rinsed my plate. I'd do dishes later, but right now, all I wanted was to curl up on the sofa and watch a movie to get my mind off things. Being humiliated at work had really brought me down.

I collapsed on the couch and heard a knock just as I reached for the remote. No one in the city knew where I lived except Charlotte, Evelyn, and the lady from HR at work. It had to be Char, because Evelyn would have called me first. For a moment, I debated whether I wanted to open the door and have company, but the knocking grew louder, so I pried myself off the couch and tossed my wet hair, heading for the door.

I pulled the door open to reveal Charlotte. In one hand, she held a dripping umbrella, in the other a bag of cheeseburgers from McDonalds, and there was a bottle of wine tucked under her arm.

"Guess who's here to rescue you from being alone after a shitty day?"

On any other day, her face would have been a welcome sight, but today I wasn't feeling it. I stepped aside, mumbling, "Come on in."

She brushed past me, leaving her umbrella by the door and heading toward the couch. The apartment was small—a bedroom, a kitchen, a bathroom, and a living room. It was a dump, but it was my home. I didn't like the place, but I liked that it was mine. The living room furniture was the remnants of a fire sale, a stained brown leather sofa, a nicked coffee table, a chipped bookshelf. All of it was purchased with the little savings I had when I moved to Chicago.

Char plopped on the old sofa which I'd had cleaned professionally with some money I scrimped together from recycling aluminum cans. I hadn't had time to do much else. The living room was painted in pale green and topped with brown shag carpeting. The window was covered over with yellowed shades, which ran down and blocked most of the light from getting in. That was well enough. If I couldn't see out, then others couldn't see in, and that was fine by me.

"You had a rough day, and I'm here to cheer you up." Charlotte smacked the sofa, and I locked the door and joined her. She set the burgers and the wine on the table and picked up the remote. "How about a chick flick while you tell me about your day?"

I shrugged. "I was about to start watching *Dirty Dancing.*"

"*Dirty Dancing*? That's your break-up movie. You told me things were okay with Dan." She dived into the bag of cheeseburgers and pulled on out, dropping it on her lap. As she surfed channels with one hand, she unwrapped the burger with the other and took a huge bite. It looked to me like she was more interested in not being alone tonight than comforting me, but after such a crappy dinner, I didn't care. I grabbed a burger and dug in too.

Our ritual of chick-flicks and wine would have to change, but even telling Charlotte about the baby seemed like a massive feat. So, I started with the small things. "I didn't say things were fine. I said it's another story and I'd bring that up later."

Charlotte chewed loudly and nodded. "Go on," she said with her mouth full. She set the burger on the wrapper sprawled on her lap and wiped her hands on her pants, then grabbed the wine bottle. She'd hit play on *Dirty Dancing* and the opening credits were rolling. "Oh, God," she said after swallowing, "I forgot glasses."

"I—" I started to protest, but she was on her feet, racing to the kitchen before I got the words out. I shrank back, nibbling the burger. I had a feeling the grease would make my stomach turn, but I ate it anyway. It was the best thing I'd eaten this week.

"Here," she said, pouring a glass full of wine from the bottle and thrusting it toward me. I took it, but I set it on the table and ate more of the burger.

"Now, tell me what's up."

As she sat, the couch jostled. I felt a bit queasy and decided to take it easy on the burgers. "Well, today was bad because of the guys being rude, but…"

"But what?" She picked up my wine glass and put it in my hand again. "Drink. You'll feel better." She gulped her wine, eyeing me as I bit my lip and looked at the half-eaten burger in the wrapper on my knee. "Drink, Em. What's wrong?"

I hesitated, my chest so constricted I thought I was having an asthma attack, and I didn't have asthma. Telling my best friend I screwed up was probably harder than telling my own parents, mostly because I still cared what she thought.

"Why aren't you drinking? You love this brand of wine."

I looked up at her and sighed. "I can't."

"Why? Are you on something else? Medication? You are sick?"

"No, Char, I can't drink with you because I'm pregnant." I set the glass down, ready for the lecture.

"Shut up!" Her eyes grew wide, eyebrows so high they almost touched her hairline. "You're serious? This isn't a joke?"

I shrugged again. "Dead serious."

She downed her full glass of wine and set it on the table, laying the cheeseburger next to it. "And he dumped you over that?" She clicked her tongue. "Girl, you can sue. You don't have to put up with this. That man has a responsibility to his—"

"No!" I took a deep breath and huffed it out. "No, I'm not suing. And no, he didn't dump me over it."

"Then why did he dump you?" She looked confused, and I felt to blame for that. Every boy I'd ever gotten dumped by—which were very few—had left me in a downward spiral of watching *Dirty Dancing* on repeat for weeks. It was only natural for her to assume he dumped me based on my movie choice.

"He didn't dump me, Char."

"Why are you watching *Dirty Dancing* then?" Charlotte took my glass of wine and sipped it. I didn't mind. I wasn't going to partake.

The couch squeaked as I shifted my weight. I laid the burger on the table and curled my knees into my chest. "When I asked him about having a family, he said he didn't see himself as a father."

"Oh, my God, you haven't told him? How long have you known?"

"A few weeks." I felt tears welling up in my eyes as I squeezed my legs. With my chin firmly planted on my knee, I said, "I don't know how to tell him. What if he's angry? What if he thinks I'm out for his money, or that I did this on purpose? God, Char, I was so excited about finally meeting a man who was interested in me and with whom I am seriously compatible. I wasn't thinking. We had sex so many times in his office and never used protection."

"So you know it's his?" She unfolded the wrapper on her burger and continued eating, chewing loudly.

"Yes, of course it's his. I haven't had sex with anyone else since I came to the city." Tucking my head down, I let the tears fall. Daniel meant so much to me. I didn't know how I'd do this without him. Sure, I could get a different job, make a living, support myself, but adding a baby to the mix would be difficult. How would I save enough money to pay the bills while I was off work for weeks on maternity leave? And how would I afford childcare I could trust?

"God, you need to tell him. Emily, this is no joke. You need proper prenatal care, screening… How are you going to afford that? Unless you have an—"

"No. I'm not aborting my baby." I gritted my teeth and looked up at her. It would be the first thing my parents demanded of me. I couldn't believe my own best friend would suggest it.

"Okay," she said, dropping the burger and holding her hands up defensively. "I'll never say it again. I'm just telling you if you don't tell him, you're going to really struggle. Babies are expensive."

"I know…" I mumbled, tucking my chin again. Babies cost a lot of money, but the cost wasn't just financial. Having this baby might just cost me my relationship. But one thing was for certain. Even if Dan didn't want the baby, I was keeping it. No one would change my mind about that.

18

DANIEL

After several meetings, I realized that my morning coffee had never arrived on my desk as usual. For the past two weeks, ever since Michael embarrassed Emily, I'd had nothing but long workdays and exhausting business dinners. I knew Emily was disappointed. She'd been down and noncommunicative. I felt bad that she had been nudged to the periphery, but sometimes, work got like this and there was nothing I could do to change that.

I'd just hung up the call with Wexler and Main, a competing firm now joining us in a class-action suit over privacy concerns with a tech giant, and my head was throbbing. If I didn't get caffeine soon, I would have a blinding headache that wouldn't go away. I pressed the intercom button on my phone, the chime ringing out. "Emily, could I get my coffee, please?"

A few seconds passed and she didn't respond, so I pushed the button again. "Emily? My coffee, please?" I gave her the benefit of the doubt that maybe she was on a call or something, but when she didn't respond the second time, I dialed her extension. She didn't pick up.

Frustrated, I stood and strolled over to my office door, pulling it open. I looked out at her desk to find it was empty. Her chair was pushed in, the computer screen dark, not turned on today. Her purse wasn't on the shelf beneath the desk, and there was no sweater draped over the back of the chair, which confused me. I glanced at my watch. It was past eight a.m. She should have been in hours ago.

Emily hadn't called to let me know she wasn't coming in, and I hadn't heard from Olivia either, so I headed to Olivia's office. When I peeked in the window, I noticed she was on a call, so I knocked quietly. After a few minutes, her voice called out, "Come in." I pushed the door open and stood in the doorway.

"Hey, did Emily call you? She's not at her desk." I leaned on the door jamb, keeping my hand on the doorknob.

"Yeah, sorry." Olivia cleared her throat and grimaced. "She called before seven, said she was sick. I was going to let you know and then got wrapped up in that conference call with Japan and the Maxell Thurman case. I apologize."

"No, that's okay." I started to leave but stuck my head back in the door. "Did she sound sick? I mean, do you think she needs anything?" My heart was on my sleeve, and I didn't care. If any one of the partners sympathized with my feelings for Emily, it was Olivia or Ben.

"Yeah, she sounded really tired and down. I'm not sure what's wrong. She didn't say. Do you want me to call her and follow up? Maybe I can send some flowers." She held her hand over her phone receiver, poised to follow my commands.

"No, that's okay. Do me a favor and have Jill cancel my morning meetings. I'm going to pick up a few things and stop by Emily's house to make sure she's okay."

"Sure thing, sir." Olivia was already dialing Jill's extension as I retreated out the door. I realized I had no clue where Emily lived, our relationship mostly centered around work, my place, and the two restaurants we'd had lunch or dinner at. I felt bad for that too. I was horrible at relationships, apparently.

I headed back to my office and sat down behind my computer. My fingers went to work searching employee personnel files for her information. I got the address and typed it into a message to my driver as well as instructions to pick me up and a few stops to make, then I took my wallet and phone and headed down to the ground floor where my limo was already waiting out front.

The line at the café where I planned to buy some soup was wrapped around the building, so I passed on that, heading instead to a coffee shop. At least I could get rid of my headache and buy her a cup of her own favorite brew. I was in and out in under fifteen minutes and on my way to Emily's apartment. I had no idea her commute across town was so long. She probably took public transportation, which was appalling to me, the idea of sitting next to common strangers and beggars on a train for thirty minutes, but I had been pampered my entire life.

By the time my driver pulled up in front of the building, I'd gained a whole new understanding of Emily that I never had a clue about. Her apartment building stood between two condemned buildings, burnt out by fire years ago and never restored. Their ownership was probably tied up in legal red tape or something. Across the street were buildings with graffiti, a computer repair shop, and a laundromat. Both had bars on the windows, which boasted of the crime rate in this neighborhood.

I shuddered at the thought of living in such horrible conditions, but I gave Emily the benefit of the doubt. She was smart—smart enough to make her own decisions. And the location of one's dwelling shouldn't reflect negatively on their value as a person, but I couldn't help but feel a bit odd, as if she'd kept this from me somehow.

I made my way to the building carrying the cups of coffee and a paper sack from the drug store where I'd purchased some pain and fever medication. There was no doorman, only a metal-framed glass door with the lock mechanism broken off it. The elevator had an *Out of Order* sign on it, so I climbed the three flights of stairs to her floor and looked for three-oh-nine. The carpet in the hallway was stained, sticky too as I walked across it.

When I found her door, I knocked, not knowing what to expect when I entered. My heart pounded in my chest as I waited for a response. After several seconds, I heard shuffling from inside and the sound of locks being undone. The door creaked open, revealing a dimly lit apartment. The curtains were drawn shut, and the only source of light came from a flickering lamp in the corner.

"Em, Olivia said you called in sick. I brought you this." I held out the coffee and drugs.

She stood in front of me, disheveled and pale. Her eyes were sunken in as if she'd been sleeping, but she didn't look sick. She took the coffee and medicine from my hands, her fingers trembling as she did so. "Thank you," she whispered, her voice hoarse.

I followed her into the apartment, taking in the surroundings. Second-hand furniture that had seen better days framed in the living space, separating the open-concept kitchen from the lounge area. A short hallway to the right was dark, a door on either side, likely the bathroom and bedroom. Emily shuffled to the kitchen counter and set the bag down, then turned toward me, hugging her coffee in her hands.

"You didn't have to come out." She wore a stained T-shirt and old gym shorts that looked like they belonged to another man. Her face still sported the mascara she'd worn yesterday, now a strange smudge of smokey eyes and clumps on her lashes.

"You're sick?" I leaned against the kitchen counter, and it moaned under my weight. Part of me wondered if the paper-thin walls would collapse if I put weight on them.

"Just feeling off today." She held her hand to her stomach. "Didn't want to share germs with anyone." The way she looked down at the coffee cup made me think she was lying, but I didn't pry. Everyone deserved a mental health day once in a while, and she'd been really depressed. I'd have been depressed, too, if I lived in conditions like this.

"I'm sorry the place is such a mess," she continued, setting her cup down. She grabbed the few plates and cups that were in her sink and stuffed them into the dishwasher, then dried her hands. I didn't think the place looked messy, just rundown. The building had to be close to being condemned.

"No, it's okay. If you're not feeling good, you should lie down." I gestured to the couch, and she nodded, picking up her coffee and heading that direction. I followed her, floorboards creaking under my feet as I went. The room smelled like old tobacco and mildew, neither scent pleasant, though she probably had gone nose blind within the first week of living here. I knew she wasn't a smoker, so it had to have been the previous tenant.

"You didn't have to check in on me. I'm fine, really." Emily plopped onto the couch and sipped her coffee, and I sat, sinking into the oversized cushion a little more than I'd have liked. The springs beneath the leather had given way a long time ago, by the looks of it. My heart wrenched in my chest. Emily didn't deserve to live in conditions like this. She was too smart, too driven.

"I care about you a lot, Em. I wanted to make sure you're okay. You've been down a lot lately, and I didn't want you to think I didn't notice."

She looked down at the coffee and shrugged. "I'm sorry. I'm okay."

"Anything you want to talk about?" I asked, and she squirmed.

"No, that's alright." She sipped the coffee again, and I could tell she was using it as a means to cover her unease. "Thank you for stopping by."

"Of course."

Seeing how she was uncomfortable, I changed the subject and talked about work. We discussed a few cases she'd been helping me with, the briefings and filings I had to organize. I hated that our conversation had been reduced to only work topics, but I knew those topics were safe and wouldn't upset her. Inside, however, I was feeling tense, like maybe everyone was right and I was making a mistake.

I didn't feel like that because of any reason other than her living conditions, though, so I warred with myself over what to believe. Mom was right. I was far out of Emily's league, and I could see it plainly now, but that shouldn't matter when love was present.

If only I could convince my logical mind what my heart vehemently believed. I told myself over and over, "Emily is pure as the driven snow," but my logic was winning out over my emotion.

19

EMILY

I sipped the coffee carefully, knowing I'd already thrown up three times this morning. I didn't want to be rude and leave Daniel seated on my couch while I raced to the bathroom. He seemed tense, as if he were uncomfortable in my place. It wasn't anything like his mansion of a home. My apartment was barely livable. Even I knew that, but he hadn't said a word about it.

"I really appreciate your stopping by." I hadn't expected any visitors. When I called in and told Olivia I'd be out today, she told me I should have called Daniel, but I knew this would happen—that he'd get the idea that I was a sick little waif who needed comfort. Honestly, I just wanted to melt into the couch cushions and be invisible. I was fiercely independent and knew I could take care of myself.

"It's no problem. I just wanted to make sure you were okay." The couch squeaked as he readjusted himself. The springs were broken, and I should have sat on that end because I knew it was uncomfortable, but the shock of his just walking into my dinky apartment made me not think straight.

"I have to be honest, Dan. I'm still a bit worried about us being so different. I know you said it doesn't matter, but I've seen the way you live, your house." My hands trembled as I brought the cup to my lips and sipped again. I wasn't self-sabotaging. I wasn't pushing him away. I honestly believed he would be happier with someone different, someone who wasn't about to thrust a surprise pregnancy on him. I still didn't have the guts to tell him about it, either.

"Emily, I've been over this with you. In fact, I've been over this with my parents and my partners. The differences aren't going to be what keeps us from being together." He pursed his lips and sighed. "You shouldn't worry about that."

I nodded, unsure of what that meant. I wondered if he thought something else would keep us from being together. His hands folded and unfolded in his lap, eyes scanning the room like he was watching for a flying insect so it didn't land on him. I could tell something was bothering him. I hated that he was uncomfortable in my place because there was nothing I could do about the conditions. Even on the decent salary the firm paid me, this was all I could afford. The city was expensive.

"You think something is going to keep us from being together?" I asked, not sure I wanted to hear his answer.

"The only thing I can foresee that would prevent me from being with you is a lie." His eyes shifted, focusing on me instead of the invisible insect. "I can get through any difficult truth, but lies… they're deal breakers."

I swallowed hard, hiding it behind the cup of coffee I brought to my lips again. I held the cup there, pretending to sip but knowing if another drop of this coffee hit my stomach, I'd definitely throw up. I wondered if he knew, or how he'd have figured out that I was pregnant. I'd been very careful. Only Char knew about the baby, and she'd never go behind my back like that. All I could do is nod in agreement and blink back the tears of guilt I had welling up. I had already lied to him.

"I'm just not feeling so hot right now." It was the truth. The added weight of emotion his words had just stirred up made me feel ten times worse. Who knew that feeling strong feelings would make morning sickness worse?

"Do you know what it is?" He leaned toward me, concerned. His hand lifted the paper cup from my grasp and set it on the table, then he pressed his hand to my forehead. "You don't feel warm."

"I wasn't' around anyone who was sick…" I was careful not to lie directly, though I knew the lie of omission would haunt me the rest of the day.

"You've just been nauseous?" His eyes studied me, and I thought for sure he was going to ask me if I was pregnant, but he didn't. I nodded and he said, "Probably just a bug. It's going around, I hear." He stood, taking the cup of coffee and heading for the kitchen. "You probably shouldn't drink this if you're sick in the stomach. You'll make it worse. I'll go out and get you soup. That will help."

"No," I blurted, standing up. I hugged my arms over my stomach and followed him to the kitchen, where he took the lid off the cup and poured the coffee down the drain. "I, uh… I'm going to make an appointment and see the doctor." *Eventually…* I added in my head, so it wasn't a lie. "I'll just run through a drive-through and get my own soup."

"Suit yourself," he said, turning to me. He set the empty cup on the counter then took me by the arms and kissed my forehead. "I'm really sorry you're not feeling well. If there is anything I can do at all, you call me. I'll come right away."

"I should be fine. Hopefully, back at work tomorrow."

Daniel's eyes did another sweep of my apartment and then rested on my face. "Are you sure you're happy here? I mean, the living conditions…" His voice trailed off, and he looked away, then hurriedly said, "I'm not judging. I'm just asking. Don't you want something better?"

I shrugged and looked around. "I grew up really poor, Dan." The broken, stained furniture had been my prized possessions when I moved in here because they were mine. My first furniture in my very own place. It was what I could afford, and I felt like a queen because I was doing it on my own.

"I lived in very meager means for a long time. It wasn't until about a year before I moved to Chicago that my parents' business took off. I remember times where we didn't even have money to buy groceries and had to go to a food pantry for help."

I turned back to him and forced a smile. "I'm not a billionaire like you, but I provide for myself. I know it's not fancy and that things could be nicer, but it's mine. You know? And I'm proud that I can live in this expensive city and be on my own."

There was an awkward silence before I took his hand. "Don't leave yet?" I asked, and he laced his fingers through mine. "Can you just hold me for a second?"

"Yeah, I can do that." His agreement seemed neither positive nor negative, but I felt like maybe he'd have rather left. I led him to my bedroom, where I folded back the covers of my unmade bed and climbed in. Dan kicked off his shoes and laid his suit coat on the foot of the bed and lay down next to me. I didn't know if this would be one of the last times I would get to enjoy his arms around me, so I soaked up every second of it. The scent of his cologne, the way he brushed his thumb across the back of my hand.

I said nothing. He did the same. We lay there until I was almost dozing and Dan got a call. He reached in his pocket and pulled it out. I saw the caller ID said Grace's name and knew he had to leave before he even cleared his throat.

"I... uh... I have to take this." Daniel pulled away from me leaving me chilled and shoved his feet into his shoes. "I'll check on you later, okay?" I nodded, and he left without another word, forgetting his suit coat.

I curled into a ball and hugged the comforter to myself. It was obvious how much I struggled. He had to have seen it. And the way he acted told me he was having second thoughts. All this before he even knew I was pregnant, which didn't bode well for me when I had to tell him about the baby.

I started to cry. In fact, I cried so hard just thinking about how angry he would be with me that my stomach started to cramp. Fear gripped me—raising this baby alone without him, him breaking up with me because I lied and hadn't told him right away. Guilt and shame washed over me, sucking me in and spitting me out until I was running to the toilet to vomit for the fourth time today.

It hurt, the acid in my throat, the dry heaving when the only thing that came up were the few swallows of coffee I'd drunk. My head hurt. It felt like my eyes would pop out of my head, but I hovered over that toilet, sobbing and retching. I had to tell him, even if it killed me. I just didn't know how to do it.

20

DANIEL

I t was a pleasant enough day, cool but calm. When Mom invited me for brunch, I almost dismissed the invitation as another event to avoid, but when she said Nick and Ginny were coming, I decided I'd go. Now I sat around the wrought-iron table on their back patio listening to Nick talk about how successful his business was. Ginny, eight months pregnant, sat across from me, chewing her food quietly. She appeared to not be as pleased with Nick's business, though I understood. She'd rather have him more available for family time.

"Anyway, things have really taken off and I'm really excited about it." Nick plunged his fork into the waffles he had selected to eat, and Ginny's head drooped.

"I'm really proud of you, son," Dad said, sipping his coffee. "You've done really well for yourself like Daniel here. His name is on just about every billboard in the city." He raised his cup as if to toast and winked at me. "Daniel is on track to be the biggest name in law in this country. I don't doubt that he'll be arguing cases at the Supreme Court one day."

I shrugged, bouncing my eyebrows up and down in one short movement. I hadn't even considered pushing a case that far, but the thought of it didn't intimidate me. Still, my mind had been on other things lately. My focus today was getting through brunch and perhaps calling Emily to see if she'd like to have dinner.

"Yes, Nick. Daniel is doing very well." Mom eyed Dad. "But we're really proud of you too. The sports industry is just as important to the economy as law. And you own the fastest-growing sporting goods brand in the country. So that's to be commended."

Mom always had to bolster Nick's ego. I was more like my father, chasing law and doing good for others. Nick was always like Mom, free spirited and happy. Not that Dad wasn't happy. It was just that no one ever saw him happy. I blamed that on the fact that he worked so much.

I had found myself falling into that same trap, not being happy, until Emily came along. It seemed she was all I thought about anymore, even days after seeing her apartment and wondering if everything Michael and my parents had said was true. She had become so important to me, it affected my entire day. When she was down or upset, I was moody and snapped at people.

"So, Daniel, how are things going?" Nick took a drink of his milk and nodded at me, pointing his fork. "You seem a bit happier than normal. Have you met someone?"

I glanced at Mom, who rolled her eyes, then Dad, who looked down at his empty plate, eggs and bacon already devoured. I wondered if it was a baited question, if they had put Nick up to asking it. Ginny's head was still down, maybe an indicator that they had.

"Yeah," I mumbled. "I have."

He furrowed his brow. "You don't seem happy to tell me." His smirk told me what I needed to know. Mom and Dad had definitely told him to ask. I breathed out a heavy breath and braced myself for the next twenty minutes of lectures that were about to start. Then I looked up and made eye contact with him.

"Her name is Emily. She is a wonderful woman. She has a master's in business management from UC Berkeley. She grew up in a small town, but she moved to the city to start her career." I smiled to myself, thinking of how sweet her heart was, how kind and caring. "She's a little sassy at times, but she has a big heart. And she is very smart."

"Big heart, small wallet," Mom said snarkily. Nick's gaze bounced from my face to Mom's. "Tell him what she does for a living, Daniel."

My father wisely stayed out of things, drinking his coffee and staring at his lap. He knew I'd fly off the handle if everyone ganged up on me. Ginny gave me a look of compassion. She'd been at the receiving end of this once. She knew how it felt.

"She is my assistant," I said dryly.

Nick started laughing. He laughed so hard he almost spilled his milk because he doubled over, then he cleared his throat and his voice sobered. I wasn't laughing with him. He sat straighter and glowered at me. "You mean you're serious? You're banging your secretary and you call that dating? That's just an affair, buddy."

"Shut up, Nick." I dropped my napkin across my plate, ready to stand up and walk off, but Ginny chimed in, calming me.

"She sounds nice." Her smile settled my heart a bit, but I was still angry.

"Nice isn't what Daniel needs." Mom scowled at me. "The girl is just plain destitute. We had her checked out. Can you believe she lives in Rodgers Park?" She sounded disgusted. I didn't even want to look at her, so I stared at my plate. "An assistant... not a secretary. And she is twelve years younger than him." Mom spat the words out like an accusation in a criminal trial. Well, she could me guilty for all I cared. Every time she spoke about Emily like this, I got angrier. It made me want Emily more.

"Dan, that's crazy. You used to date..." He snapped his fingers in the air, his tiny brain trying to conjure up the name. "What was her name?"

"Keri Davidson," Mom said, supplying the name I never wanted to hear again.

"Damn, yeah. She's listed among the wealthiest women in the city now. Dude, how could you lower your standards?" Nick shoved another bite of food into his mouth, and I wanted to cram the fork down his throat with it. How could he take their side after what they did to Ginny when he was dating her?

"Keri and I didn't see eye to eye." That was an understatement, but I was pinned down. "And I think I need to use the restroom." I stood, excusing myself, and went to the toilets where I hid for a few moments after reliving my bladder. I reached for my phone, checking notifications. There were none from Emily, who was the only person I wanted to speak with at that moment, so I returned to the table after washing my hands.

I was surprised to see that only Ginny remained seated. I heard Dad and Nick chatting around the corner where they usually smoked their cigars after eating. Mom was nowhere in sight. Ginny looked up at me expectantly. I lowered myself into my seat and she whispered, "I think Emily sounds great."

The smile I gave her was genuine. It was refreshing to hear that at least one person in my life supported me, even if I did have my doubts about it all. "Thanks, Gin. I knew you'd be the only one to understand."

"Tell me more about her?" she asked, leaning on the table with her elbows. She planted her chin on the heel of her hand and grinned at me.

"Well, she's funny. She knows how to make me laugh. And like I said, she's so smart. I believe she's really going places, just like Nick has." I thought of how my parents once doubted he'd do anything with his life because he refused to go to law school. "When she smiles, she has a dimple right here." I pointed at my cheek. "And she's beautiful, so beautiful."

I couldn't help feeling a bit lovestruck, though I knew Ginny wouldn't mind. She was a helpless romantic if there ever was one. Emily and Ginny would get along great, once they met.

"I'm really happy for you, Daniel. Your parents are so strict. I knew they hated me when I met Nick, and I was happy that you and Nick stood up for me. I'm glad they've come around now too and stopped treating me so badly. So I totally understand how you're feeling. Just don't get too upset with them. They only want what's best for you. Okay?" She reached out and touched my hand lightly. I nodded.

"Yeah, I understand that. I'm just frustrated that they seem hell-bent on destroying what I have with Emily before we even really get started. I just want a bit of space to figure out life for myself. I'm nearly forty years old." I chuckled. "You'd think they would want me to leave them alone to live their life at this point, but they still hover over me."

Ginny pulled away and tucked her hands in her lap, though she snickered. "Well, I think you're on the right track. You're successful. You provide for yourself. You aren't entirely a slob."

I laughed with her. "I try to be clean."

"And most of all, you have a good heart. You don't judge people based on the way they look or the way they dress. Their financial status isn't important to you. And I think that makes you okay in my book."

I thought of how Emily's apartment was so rundown that I cringed at the thought of sitting on her couch, and Ginny's words made me feel guilty. I had judged Emily, not outrightly, but in my heart. Part of me was discouraged and even made suspicious by how she hadn't told me how much she struggled financially. Or maybe to her, that wasn't struggling.

It remained a possibility that Emily was doing really well for herself, and I just hadn't seen how she grew up. I didn't know how to feel about that. I didn't want to be a judgmental asshole, but I also wanted to know that she wasn't just out for my money. She'd never done anything that would cause me to believe she was. That was all something planted in my head by Michael and my parents.

"You look troubled." Ginny's kind eyes pulled me in.

"Something my mom said, about Emily being a gold digger." I didn't really want to get into this with anyone, but Ginny seemed compassionate, not at all like the rest of my family.

"You're worried she's using you?"

"Yeah."

"Has she asked you for money? Asked you to pay her bills?" Her eyebrows rose, and I saw sympathy in her eyes.

"No, not at all. It's been a pretty normal relationship so far."

"And did you pursue her, or the other way around?"

I had to think about that because even though I put the moves on her first, it felt like it was more a mutual interest. "I don't really know. I do know I asked her to kiss me first."

"Well, then, I think you sort of have your answer. Just trust your heart. Don't let other people influence your thoughts. If you love her, you go get what you want. If you feel hesitant, then wait and see."

Mom appeared in the door carrying a glass of wine and a bottle, and that was my cue to leave. I stood and nodded. "Thanks, Ginny." She shook her head and then looked back down at her plate. I turned to Mom. "I'm headed out. I'll give you a call later this week, okay?"

"Yes, Daniel. Run away before your brother can talk any sense into you. Just be careful out there. The world is full of evil women hoping to swindle you out of your heart."

I rolled my eyes and headed into the house and out toward the front. I wanted to call Emily now, not wait another second. After talking with Ginny, I knew what I wanted. I wanted to see her, to tell her I loved her and it didn't matter where she came from or what her desire for me even was. I wanted her no matter what.

21

EMILY

I sat in the booth near the back of the restaurant, waiting. Evelyn was late, which wasn't normal for her, but it gave me time to think. I ordered for both of us because we both enjoyed the same things. After weeks of thought, I wasn't as angry about her telling my parents about me and Dan dating. After all, she was my sister and she did care about me. And it had taken the stress of my telling them off my shoulders, so that was a bonus too. I hadn't been around for their initial reaction. What I'd gotten from Mom was just a well-thought-out speech. Probably better that way.

Tonight's "sister dinner" would be an opportunity for me to really just be with Evelyn and try to relax a little. When Charlotte came over, she just wanted to sit and talk about the baby and my decisions. I needed space from that conversation tonight, so I hadn't invited her to come.

The place wasn't very busy. It was a rainy night. When that happened, people stayed home and had delivery services bring their food. I had ventured out into the rain because it reminded me of back home, walking where I wanted to go even if it was raining. I had a good umbrella, and for the most part, I stayed dry, but when Evelyn walked in with soggy feet, I could tell she wasn't as happy to enjoy the melancholy weather as I was.

"God, it's awful out there," she said, flopping into the seat. She stashed her umbrella in the same place I'd hidden mine, under the table. "You ordered?"

"Yeah, the grilled chicken Caesar salad." I pushed her glass of water toward her. "That's what we always get."

"Yes, it is…" She huffed out a sigh and reached under the table. "My feet are soaked. I'm going to have prunes for toes. I think it's flooding out there."

"I'm sorry that happened." I felt guilty, which she knew I would. Even though the rain wasn't my fault and she could have worn galoshes like me, it was my fault. Always my fault with Evelyn.

"Ah, well, at least you're dry." She smiled, reminding me of my mother so much.

"So, how is the family?" I asked, trying to change the subject. Tonight was about relaxing. I had to remind myself a few times so I didn't get too irritated by Evelyn's behavior.

"Same old, same old." She pushed some damp hair out of her eyes and looked up at me with a stern expression. "Have you told your boss to buzz off yet?"

I stared at my empty place setting and let my shoulders droop. "I was hoping we could just have a good evening, Eve. I don't want to argue."

"I'm not trying to argue, Em. I care about you."

The waitress walked up with our salads, causing a distraction I hoped would be enough to dissuade Evelyn from pressing the issue. The woman sat our food down and asked, "Does it look okay?"

"Looks delicious, thank you," Evelyn told her and unwrapped her silverware.

"Looks good." I smiled at the kind older woman, and she nodded.

"Need anything, just flag me down."

And then the distraction was gone, and I was left facing my brutish older sister. She meticulously lined her silverware up on the right-hand side of her bowl, then snapped the napkin and draped it across her lap before sipping her water and picking up her fork.

"So, are you going to tell me or not?" she asked again, and I shrugged.

I unrolled my silverware and pulled out my fork. I was famished, ready to eat my entire salad and hers. I stabbed a crouton and put it in my mouth, crunching it to delay having to answer, but Evelyn knew my procrastination was answer enough. I was surprised, however, when her voice was calm as she continued. Not the expected harsh lecture.

"You know, Em, when you moved to Chicago, I had really high hopes for you. I still do." She took a bite and chewed it, speaking only after she had swallowed. I had a bite too. It was better than I expected. "This whole business with your boss, though, I'm worried."

Evelyn was never calm like this when I was doing something she didn't approve of. Not when I asked to move to California to go to school—which never happened—or when I wanted to do a six-month trip to Eastern Europe for an exchange program. It was like she thought of me as her own daughter, not her sister. I was always at the receiving end of some lectures. But tonight, she was collected and patient, which made me want to at least try to get along and listen instead of arguing.

"Emily, this guy is so much older than you. Even if he's not abusing his power to get you to date him, he's just too old. What if you get pregnant and he pressures you to marry him just because you're having his baby? What if you end up not liking him that much? You get married, have his kid. Ten years down the line, you're still in your thirties wanting to have a life, and he's pushing fifty and ready to have a heart attack and die."

"Oh, I don't think that will happen." I plunged my fork into my salad and speared a bite of it.

"Look what happened to Charlotte's dad. Died at forty-eight. Massive heart attack." Evelyn looked at me with concern. "Honey, I love you. I'm trying to watch out for you. Even if he doesn't die, a man who is that much older than you will slow down faster. He'll be tired, ready for bed by eight p.m. while you're wanting to enjoy a movie. You'll want to be out hiking and running, and he'll have lower back issues."

I stared at my salad, feeling less hungry than before. Everything she was saying made sense, but I cared about Daniel. She didn't know I was already pregnant, and I had no intention of telling her, but that doubled the heavy emotion I was already feeling as she continued.

"Say you have a kid now. In twenty years, you'll be in your forties, still able to live an incredible life, and he'll be pushing sixty." She frowned at me, and my eyes brimmed with tears. "Babe, think about it. A man that good-looking who is that old? Why hasn't he settled down? I bet he's told you he never found 'the one'. Hasn't he?"

"He never said that," I told her, but I had never asked. It never occurred to me to ask him. I was just happy he took an interest in me.

"Let me educate you, Emily." Evelyn put her fork down and wiped her hands. "He probably has a million mistresses just waiting to be the next one bent over his desk. He can have any woman he wants without any restrictions. He's hot, he's powerful, and he's single." She ticked the list off on her fingers, and I blinked, tears streaming down my face. "He isn't married because he's a player, and he's playing you too."

"I don't think so..." I shook my head, not ready to believe that quite yet. I couldn't believe that. To agree with her would be to crush my own heart. Daniel would never do that to me. He loved me. I loved him. Right?

"Do you have proof otherwise?" she asked, picking her fork back up.

I could have asked Jill, but Jill was married. She had a family. She wasn't the type to have an affair. As far as I knew, she'd been his secretary for years before me. All I could do was shrug at Evelyn and let my shoulders fall again.

"Trust me. You need to break it off. Let me and Charlotte find you a respectable guy closer to your age."

"No, thank you," I mumbled. Even if I was ready to break it off with Dan, I wasn't ready to date anyone else. Not for a long time. Not with the baby coming.

Evelyn finished her salad, but I wasn't interested in mine. She changed the subject, maybe realizing how emotional it made me, and we talked about her job and her frustration with her husband.

By the time I left the restaurant, it wasn't raining anymore. I wanted to call Daniel, to ask him again if he was serious about me. I wanted reassurance and encouragement, but the thought of lying to him about the baby stopped me from dialing his number. He'd said lying was the one thing that would break us up, and I had a huge secret.

I scolded myself for having not told him about the baby yet. My mind was so overwhelmed with fear that this was all some game to him that I just didn't know what to think. I wanted to trust that he was being real with me and not playing me like a pawn. But now, after everything my sister said to me, I feared the worst again. Only, the place I knew I could get comfort was the very place I was afraid to go.

As I walked toward my apartment, I pulled my phone out. I needed a few days out of the city to think about things. Going home to Monroe County was the only option. Staying here in Chicago would mean work and interacting with Daniel. It would mean him popping into my apartment to see me—if he hadn't been disgusted by it in the first place. Or it would mean him inviting me out, taking me to dinner and wanting me to go to his place. I just wanted to think.

"Em?" Mom said when the phone rang through to her number.

"Mom... Can I come home? I mean, just for the weekend. Maybe a little longer? I want to visit. I miss you guys."

"Oh, honey, yes, you can come home any time. Your room is just like you left it." She paused, and I sighed. "Is everything okay?"

I kicked a stone on the sidewalk. It skidded into the street, and I watched a car run over it. "I'm just lonely. I want to be around you and Daddy. Is that okay?"

"Of course, Emily. You are welcome here any time. You let me know the arrangements, and I'll make sure we are at the airport to pick you up."

"Okay, Mom. Thank you."

"You're welcome, sweetheart. I hope you're feeling okay." Mom was prying, like always, but I wouldn't get into it over the phone. This would be my weekend of reckoning. I could already tell. But a lecture from my parents was better than finding out I had been played by the only man who ever wanted me.

"I'm okay now. I just need to come home and rest for a few days."

We said our goodbyes, and I hung up, but the feeling of torment in my chest didn't go away. And when the rain started back up, I didn't use my umbrella. I wanted to feel something—anything, other than sadness or fear. The cold droplets on my skin made me feel alive for a moment, connected to the rest of the world instead of on my own island of pain.

I trudged forward as the heavens poured down, drenching me, and I thought of Daniel. Charming, charismatic, handsome, powerful, everything that drew me in. Now they were things I was skeptical about, even suspicious. I didn't know what to believe except that I loved him more than life itself, and I wanted a life with him—a family. My deepest fears preyed on me, spurred on by Evelyn's concerned talk. How would I raise this baby by myself? Because there was no way I was getting rid of it. Abortion or adoption—neither one was an option for me.

If Evelyn was right and Daniel was playing me, this baby was the only thing I had left of him. There was no way I was giving that up.

DANIEL

The entire day had dragged on—a few days, actually. When Emily left a voicemail on my work phone that she was going to her parents' house for the weekend, after days of almost zero interaction here at work and no time with her outside of work, I felt discouraged. I had hoped we would have time this weekend to sit and talk. After talking with Ginny about her, I felt more strongly that not only should a conversation be had, but soon. Now it would have to wait.

"And you think diversifying is the best way?" Chuck Hamlin sat across from me with his folder open in front of him. My last meeting of the day, and I wished it were over already.

"I'm not an investor. I'm a lawyer. But I do think having all your eggs in one basket isn't a good idea. I think you should definitely diversify. I also strongly advise you to consider filing your S-Corp because sole proprietorship LLCs are risky. You are liable for every single cent of taxes you owe. If you get a S-Corp and your business goes under, you can dissolve the company and that's that." I'd told him this many times, but the man refused to open his small company up to what he called "micromanaging board members".

"Yes, yes. Well, I'll consider your advice there." He slapped the folder shut and stood up, thrusting his hand out. "Thanks again for your advice, Dan. I'll be in touch." I shook his hand, and he turned and strutted toward the door.

I would never understand why people put me on retainer at three hundred dollars an hour if they were going to refuse my advice, but I'd take their money anyway. They paid me for my professional opinion and the ability to file their legal documents on their behalf. It did not reflect on my reputation if they ignored me.

I sat back down and rubbed my forehead. I had a headache and needed an aspirin. With only a half hour left in the day, I would stick it out and grab a cat nap when I got home, but I had a client dinner this evening too. I wanted a break. I wanted to see Emily. I was sick of running myself ragged on this exercise wheel I called a job. I toyed with the idea of planning a weekend away, just me and Emily, but with her taking a long weekend this weekend, I knew she wouldn't be able to afford it, and there would be no pulling strings to get her extra vacation time. Michael wouldn't allow that.

I sighed and tried to push Emily out of my mind. I couldn't afford distractions right now. I had a deadline to meet and the client dinner to attend. As I stared blankly at the computer screen, my phone vibrated in my pocket. I pulled it out hoping it was from Emily, but it was only a reminder of my dental cleaning appointment on Monday morning.

I laid my head back and closed my eyes, the coolness of the vinyl chair on my back, the warmth of the sun on my face. For a moment, the pain throbbing at my temples subsided and I let the tension out of my shoulders. When the weekend was over, I would invite Emily to dinner. We would chat about all of my concerns, and I'd have a chance to tell her what I really wanted. If we couldn't get away for the weekend, I'd ask her to come stay at my place for a few days or the week. At least we'd be together every night.

"Mr. Jacobs?" Olivia's voice over my intercom startled me. I was expecting Jill, since she was filling in for Emily while she was gone.

Then I remembered today was the day Jill had to leave early to get her kids from school for swimming lessons.

I pressed the button and said, "Yeah, Olivia..."

"Sir, you have a visitor."

Normally, my "visitors" were announced by name. I wasn't aware of any meetings or commitments. Jill would have advised me of that earlier, so it must have been a social call. "Who is it?"

"Sir, I think you should see her." Olivia's tone was firm, and I got the hint that it was more than a social call.

"Send her in." I stood and waited, tie tucked in my jacket properly. The door opened, and Olivia peeked in briefly before a woman I didn't recognize entered.

"Thank you," she said quietly to Olivia. Then she turned to me. "Mr. Daniel Jacobs?" she asked in a clipped tone.

"Yes, I am." I remained behind my desk, my place of power. I learned a long time ago that the place of authority is relinquished when I move from behind my desk. As if I stepped down from my seat of power to deign myself in humility.

The woman looked familiar. Her cheekbones, her eyes, the way she pursed her lips. I couldn't place where I'd seen her before, but she reminded me of someone. I had a feeling I was about to find out who. Perhaps some unhappy client.

"Mr. Jacobs, my name is Evelyn Harper." She moved toward my desk, remaining standing as I was. She wore tight-fitting jeans, a red ruffled top, and red heels, and she carried a clutch-type purse.

"Ms. Harper, what can I do for you?" I gestured at the chair beside her, but she scowled at me.

"I'd rather stand, thank you."

"Alright... How can I help?" Her demeanor was cold and closed. Most clients were open, vulnerable, wanting me to help them. But Evelyn was fierce, almost angry.

"Mr. Jacobs, I'm here to speak to you about my sister, Emily Kline." Evelyn tucked her clutch under her arm and looked down her nose at me as shock smacked me across the face.

She looked familiar because she looked so much like her sister. I could see it now, the way her nose turned up at the end, the shape of her face. Their hair was a different color, but as soon as she pointed it out, I saw the resemblance. I wanted to smile, to greet her warmly, but I got the feeling she wasn't here to be social. Her jaw was set, her shoulders squared.

"I should say it's nice to meet you, but I get the feeling you don't think it is." I cleared my throat and adjusted my tie. "What is it that I can do for you, Ms. Harper?"

She stared at me through narrowed eyes, and I watched her body tense. "Mr. Jacobs, I am here to let you know that if you don't back off, leave my sister alone, my family will file a lawsuit against you and this firm. Gross abuse of power, sexual harassment, hostile work environment, and whatever else you've done. You cannot throw your weight around and pressure a naïve woman into doing your bidding."

Her words came like a kick in the gut. I had to sit down. I was winded, unable to formulate words for the moment as I reeled in shock. Sexual harassment? I had asked Emily a number of times if she wanted me to stop. I'd invited her to dinner, built what I thought was trust and a relationship.

"Ms. Harper, I'm afraid you're wrong. Emily and I are in l—"

"Are you?" she snapped, interrupting. "Or have you just thrown your weight around and bullied her? You realize she's not a city girl, right? That she doesn't know the ways of the world the way a man twelve years older than her might." Evelyn uncrossed her arms and grabbed her clutch in hand, then crossed her arms again. She was fidgeting, which meant she was either very emotionally worked up or nervous. I banked on the former. "You have no right to twist her emotions and get in her head. Shame on you."

I licked my lips. My tongue clung to the roof of my mouth. My palms were sweaty. I felt my chest constricting. "Did Emily ask you to do this? Did she send you?" I didn't know if I'd believe Emily sent this woman even if she told me she had.

"Mr. Jacobs, you've been warned. You leave her alone, or the suit will be filed. And we will hire Peterson, Baker, and Tomlin."

The names rolled off her tongue, and I clenched my jaw. I rose as she started for the door, wishing I had some retort or way of defending myself, but I had nothing. There were no words. My head spun. I couldn't believe what I heard. Why would Emily do this? I hadn't pressured her once. I watched Evelyn storm out without trying to stop her and sank into my chair again. When I dialed Emily's number, it went straight to voicemail. There was no point in leaving a message. I needed to speak to her in person about this, not over the phone.

My body felt heavy and frozen in place. Those were very strong accusations Evelyn cast at me, and all false. There was no way a court would side with the bogus claims, but it would drag my name through the mud, be hung up in litigation for months, scare potential clients, or current clients, away. This was all too much. I sank my head into my hands and rested my elbows on my knees.

Until I heard a knock at the door, and it squeaked open.

I looked up and saw Michael standing there. His expression told me he knew something. I shook my head and let my jaw drop. He moved toward my desk, jacket in one hand, draped over his shoulder.

"Emily's sister?" he said as he sat down.

"Yeah..." I mumbled.

"What did she say?"

So apparently, he didn't hear anything, but Olivia had told him who Evelyn was. I debated internally whether to tell him or not but decided he had to know. If this threat was real, there was no point hiding it.

"I haven't spoken to Emily about it yet."

"Spill it, Dan." Michael tossed his jacket into the chair next to himself and scowled at me.

"Ms. Harper threatened a lawsuit against me and the firm if I don't back off from Emily." I swallowed hard, the constriction in my throat nearly choking me. "I don't know if this is Emily's doing or her family's. She said her parents were pretty controlling."

"Goddammit, Dan. I told you this would happen. You never listen to me. I literally told you this exact scenario would play out, and look at you now." His lecture continued for the next forty-five minutes, during which I tried calling Emily another dozen times, all with the same result. The calls went straight to voicemail. Either her phone was dead or she'd blocked me.

23

EMILY

I trudged through the airport terminal, following the crowd as they moved toward the main exit. The wheels on my small black suitcase clicked on the floor tiles. I was exhausted. The flight was short, but it was getting on in the evening and I hadn't slept well this week. I wasn't looking forward to the evening much because I knew Mom and Dad would want me to sit around talking. Mom would make dinner and Dad would want to show me his newest creation for work. My brain hurt just thinking about it.

They were waiting when I passed security, holding a giant sign Mom had made. It said *Welcome Home* in giant glitter letters and had hearts and smiley faces all over it. It had only been a few months, but the warm welcome felt nice. I threw my arms around her and let the suitcase sit.

"I missed you," I mumbled, already on the verge of tears. One thing I hated about being pregnant was that I was so damn emotional. Everything made me cry.

"Oh, baby, we missed you too." Mom smoothed my hair and squeezed me.

"Hey, don't hog all the hugs now, Nan." Dad nudged his way in, and I hugged him too. He smelled like pipe tobacco, but he gave the best hugs. When he let me go, he said, "Alright, let's get out of here. Traffic will be a nightmare, and I'm hungry."

I nodded and reached for my suitcase, but Dad grabbed it and headed off. Mom hooked her arm around mine and smiled. "I made pot roast and lentils. Oh, and that marble cake with caramel icing you like so much. And I got your room ready. I mean, it's exactly how you left it, but I put clean sheets on the bed and dusted a little. Gosh, I'm so glad you're home."

Mom went on about her new hobby of knitting for about twenty minutes, long after we were in the old rusty pickup truck headed down the highway. I couldn't believe Dad still had this old hunk of junk. He bought it brand-new from the factory and told everyone as long as it was running, he'd keep it. Thirty years later, it was still moving, though it had seen better days. It was comforting, curled up in the back seat with no leg room, reminiscing about being a child and riding around in his truck.

Life had changed so quickly for me when I moved to Chicago, so coming home, where life was slower and not much changed, felt comforting. I closed my eyes and hugged my knees to my chest and dozed off as we bumped over potholes. When I heard the crunch of gravel and felt the truck stop, I knew we were home. I blinked my eyes open and yawned.

"Welcome back to the land of the living," Dad joked. "I'll get your bag. You help Mom finish supper." He slammed the car door and pulled my bag out of the bed, and Mom opened the door on our side and let me out.

"You don't have to cook. You can just sit and watch. You look exhausted." She led the way, and I trailed behind her.

It was still light out, but growing dusky. The sun setting over the large barn out back where Dad kept his boat cast beautiful rays of colorful light in the sky. I noticed they'd cut down the old oak tree in the backyard. They'd been talking about it for years. I guess things did change around here a bit.

The porch still creaked when I stepped on it, and the corner drooped a little, sinking into the weeds that grew up around it. The awning sagged in the center, showing its age. Dad was so busy with work all the time that he never got around to house repairs, and it appeared to me that situation hadn't changed a bit.

"You can freshen up if you want," Mom said as we walked into the kitchen.

My stomach was upset again, probably from not having eaten all day. Morning sickness was worse when I abstained from food. I should have learned my lesson and at least had a snack, but I was too emotional. After Evelyn said all those things about Daniel at dinner yesterday, I couldn't think straight, let alone eat. I pressed my hand to my belly and sighed.

"Not feeling well?" she asked.

"Yeah, honestly, if you don't mind, I'd like to just go to bed tonight. I'm not feeling well." I leaned on the door jamb and rested my head on the wall.

"Oh, no. I hope you're not coming down with something." Mom pressed her hand to my forehead. "You don't feel warm. It's probably just motion sickness from the flight. You go on to your room and lie down. I'll bring you some soup after a bit."

"Thanks, Mom."

I turned and headed up the hallway where light streamed out of my open door onto the worn yellow carpet that had almost lost its nap. The carpet in my bedroom wasn't as worn, a light blue that Evelyn always made fun of because it was a "boy color". I didn't mind it, never did. I collapsed onto my bed and kicked my shoes off, burying myself beneath the covers. My heart was as heavy as my stomach.

The longer I thought about what my sister told me, the more I believed her. A man with that much power and money had to have so many women he didn't know what to do with. And a man that age should have found the woman he wanted to spend the rest of his life with by now, unless he had no intention of settling down, anyway. Either way, I was just another notch in his belt and I had been played.

Tears came hot and fast, drenching my green pillowcase. I had to reach into my suitcase, left by the side of my bed by Dad, to get a tissue from the small travel pack I stuffed in the outer pocket. One tissue turned into two, then another, and after a while, the entire pack was crumpled and snotty, lying in a heap on my nightstand. My eyes were heavy and ached from crying so much, and I was about to doze off when Mom shuffled in carrying a tray table and a bowl of soup. She set them on the bed next to me, and I sat up.

"That smells really good." I adjusted myself in bed so she could position the tray table over my legs and nervously glanced at the pile of soggy tissues.

"You've been crying?" she asked, perching carefully on the edge of the bed. "Honey, is everything okay?"

My shoulders slumped as I picked up the spoon and stirred the steaming soup. Ham and potato was my favorite. It always had been. But I didn't know if I could eat a single bite without throwing it up. My stomach wasn't kind about that. It didn't matter how much my tongue loved the taste. My belly didn't agree with anything I put in it some days.

"I'm okay, Mom."

"Emily, you stop lying to me this instant. You girls have always known that you can tell me anything. You've been crying. A lot, by the looks of it. Now tell me why you're crying."

It was now or never. If I didn't tell Mom, she'd find out soon enough, and then she would not only be upset that I was pregnant, but she'd also feel hurt that I didn't trust her enough to be honest with her in the beginning. I swallowed the constrictor that wrapped his slithery body around my throat and took a deep breath before I started.

"Mom, I know that you and Dad expect me to do things a certain way. I understand why you have expectations and hopes for me. And I'm sorry that I probably failed in your eyes."

"What do you mean, honey?"

"I'm pregnant." I couldn't look her in the eye. Shame washed over me—not because I was ashamed of being pregnant or because I didn't want this baby so badly. It was a shame because I knew they wanted me to have my degree, then my career, then a husband, and finally—most importantly, last on the list—a baby.

"You're what?" she asked, almost in a whisper.

"It was an accident, obviously. I wasn't careful like I should have been and I—"

"It's that old man's?"

I looked up at her, hurt at the attempt to slander Daniel by calling him old. "Mom, you realize you're older than him."

"You know what I mean, Emily. Don't avoid the question."

"Yes, Mom, Daniel is the father." Annoyed, I took a bite of soup, a bit larger than I should have, and it was hot. It burnt my tongue and I whimpered.

"Well, doesn't that just take the cake. He got you pregnant and now you've come home too. What did he do, dump you? What a real piece of—"

"Mom, stop." I spoke with my mouth full of food, and it forced her to stop speaking. She scowled at me while I chewed and swallowed. "He didn't dump me. I came home for a visit because I missed you guys and I needed some time to think about how to tell him." I stirred the soup and blew on it, hoping to cool it off enough to eat. It was a delicious distraction from my emotional wreckage.

"So you haven't even told him?" Her eyebrows rose.

"No. He doesn't know. I don't know how to tell him. How did you tell Dad you were pregnant with Evelyn?"

Her lips pursed, deepening her scowl. "Well, first of all, I was married, so it was a happy thing."

I rolled my eyes. "I should have never told you."

"Look, if you haven't said anything yet, that's better. It means you can take care of this and he'll never be the wiser."

"What do you mean?" I asked, my chest tightening.

"I mean, we'll go to the women's clinic in the morning. You have options. I think ending this now while it's very early is the best. Your whole life will be completely ruined if you keep this baby. And God forbid your father finds out." She pressed her hands to her face and sighed deeply, then dropped them.

"There is no way I'm aborting my baby, Mom."

"You don't know what you're saying. It's not even a baby yet. Okay? Just think of it like a wart you need to cut off." Mom stood, and I wanted to scream at her. "We'll go first thing in the morning. You'll see, Emily, that this is the best thing for you. I can't imagine how hard your life would be if you kept it. You'll see."

"Uh…" My brain felt like it was going to explode. Mom walked out as calmly as she walked in, and my head was spinning. How could she compare my baby to a wart that needed to be removed? That wasn't at all the reaction I had expected.

I thought she'd be angry, shout at me. Maybe call my father into the room and attempt to punish me like I was a naughty child with lectures and grounding. It almost felt like she expected this to happen and she'd thought out her reaction and a plan moving forward for just such an event. And it infuriated me.

I finished the soup and set the tray outside my door and locked it. Morning and the chance to bicker with her about this would both come soon enough. I needed sleep.

24

DANIEL

As I pushed open the door to the restaurant, I was hit with a wave of warm air and the delicious scent of cooking food. The interior was dimly lit, with soft yellow lights casting a warm glow over the space. The walls were painted a soft cream color, and various framed paintings and photographs hung on them, giving the space a cozy, inviting feel.

The sound of jazz music played softly in the background, and I could hear the chatter of customers seated at the tables. I approached the hostess stand and the petite woman standing there smiled at me.

"Good afternoon, sir. Welcome to our restaurant. How may I assist you?" she asked.

"Hi there, I'm meeting my father for lunch today. Do you have a table available?" I replied.

"Of course, sir. We have a few tables available. Would you like to be seated by the window or in the main dining area?" she asked.

"The window would be nice, please," I said.

"Alright, please follow me," she said as she led me to a table by the large windows, which let in a flood of natural light and offered a pleasant view of the outside.

I sat and waited for my father, frustrated and overwhelmed. After everything that had happened, I couldn't shake the feeling that Emily had been using me all along. It seemed like she had weaseled her way into my life to mess it up and take my money. I had tried to ignore these thoughts for months, but they had only grown stronger with time. I should have listened to Michael and my parents from the beginning.

As I waited for my father, I fiddled with my fork, trying to calm my nerves. I couldn't help but wonder what he would say when I told him what Emily's sister had said. I wasn't ready for the "I told you so" lecture. It was difficult for me to eat my words, but after having fought for her so passionately because I believed her, trusted her, this entire conversation was going to be torture.

Dad walked in, standing tall with squared shoulders. The suit he wore told me he had come from work, not the golf course or home. I watched him address the hostess, and she led him in my direction. The closer he got, the more my gut tightened. He had warned me, and I'd ignored his wisdom in favor of following my heart, and that had been a huge mistake.

"Daniel," he said, sitting. "Thank you." He nodded at the hostess, and she walked away. "How are things?" he asked, taking his napkin and draping it over his knee. I mirrored his movements, placing the black cloth napkin across my lap.

"Things have been better." I wasn't sure how to admit to him how wrong I'd been or that I was now facing a lawsuit.

"Is that right?" he asked. It was like he already knew and he was just toying with me. That thought was ridiculous. There was no way he knew anything yet, but he always had a sixth sense about things. Besides the fact that he had actually been right about Emily, so he was probably waiting for me to come crawling to him with my tail between my legs admitting my defeat. "Anything you want to talk about in particular?"

The waitress walked up to us, interrupting, much to my temporary relief.

"How are the two of you today?" she asked, pen ready to take our order.

"Fine thank you," I told her, avoiding my father's languid gaze.

"We specialize in Italian cuisine, and our chef is well known for his handmade pasta. Our special today is linguini Alfredo. Would you like to start with an appetizer?" She clicked her pen and smiled at me.

"No, thanks. Let's start with a couple of waters. I'll have a cup of coffee, black, and we'll take the special. Thank you." It was like my father to take command. He ordered for both of us without asking my consent, something he'd have done to me when I was a child. The habit never wore off.

The waitress scribbled something on her pad and shoved it in her apron pocket. "I'll be right back with those waters and your coffee." She walked away, and I was left with nothing but time to be humiliated by his reproach.

"Now, you were saying?" Dad leaned in his chair at an angle, crossing one arm over his stomach and grasping his other wrist.

"You were right." The words clawed their way out of my throat, scratching me and tearing out part of my heart with them as they left my lips. I had loved her so deeply, more than any woman I'd ever met, and she'd deceived me.

"How is that?" he asked, readjusting his silverware. He was torturing me, making me work for it. He would force me to admit with my own mouth everything that was happening because he relished the idea that I was still lesser than him.

"Her family threatened to file a lawsuit—sexual harassment, gross abuse of power, hostile work environment. You name it." I clenched my jaw and braced myself. I found myself fidgeting with the fork again. I must have gotten that from him. Two peas in a pod. Except when it came to women. I was a damn fool, easy to trick, and it happened time and again.

He said nothing, just sat there with his hand resting on the table. The silence was worse than a lecture. I wanted him to just lay into me, tell me I was stupid, yell at me, anything other than sit there staring. I squirmed in my seat, frustrated. Michael had at least shouted at me, told me what a dummy I was, but I knew the firm would back me and so would my other staff members. I'd never been anything other than ethical with them, so there was no history of my having uncouth behavior.

"Well, Son, how bad is it? Do you think they're serious?"

The question was not expected at all. I looked up at him and shrugged my shoulders. "I think her sister was very serious. She waited until the end of the day, after Emily had already told me she'd be visiting her parents for the weekend. She came into my office, told me how evil I was and that they'd sue if I didn't back off, and Emily hasn't answered a single call or text message since then." That part had sealed the deal for me.

If it was just Emily's sister speaking out of turn, why was Emily avoiding me? Refusing my calls... But because of the timing, the way things happened, and Emily's silence, I knew in my heart that it was a real threat.

"Alright, then back off." His words made my heart wrench. Back off? How did I do that when I loved her?

I wanted to call her and talk this out, find out what she was thinking. If she'd been that unhappy with me, why hadn't she told me about it? Why had she gone to her family to complain about the work environment?

"And you should get the firm to write up termination papers for her too. Make it legal. You have to show that her threats were taken seriously. Nip it in the bud before they think you're still pursuing her." Dad smiled as the waitress walked up and set two glasses of water and a cup of coffee in front of us. "Thank you, dear."

"No problem. Your meals will be out soon. You got in just before the rush." She tucked her empty tray under her arm and strolled away, and I noticed the line of folks by the hostess stand. She was right, the place would be packed in a few moments.

"Look, Dan. You didn't listen. Shame on you. But now that you know, before any damage is done, you can take action. Cut her off. Make it clear to her family that you have. Provide her a nice severance package and be done with it."

My shoulders dropped in defeat. I didn't want to do any of that because my heart was still so tangled up with emotion for her, but I knew it was the right call. I'd never had to walk away from someone I still loved. It was the hardest thing I'd ever thought of doing. But as I sat there, sipping my water, I realized that my dad was right. It was time to move on and cut my losses. Emily's behavior had shown me that she didn't want to be with me, and it was time for me to accept that and move on. If she was brash enough to scheme with her family to do this to me, then I'd force her to play her own game.

The waitress returned to deliver our food, though I wasn't hungry anymore, and as she did, a familiar face showed up. Keri Davidson stood beside me, grinning.

"Dan, I invited Keri. I thought you two could catch up a bit." Dad looked proud of himself, but I was very unhappy with him.

I felt a wave of annoyance wash over me at the sight of Keri. She was the last person I wanted to see right now, especially after the conversation I had just had with my dad about Emily. Keri and I had too much of a sour history to ever redeem it and have a future. She was always stuck up and seemed to enjoy causing drama wherever she went. I had no interest in catching up with her.

"Thanks for inviting her, Dad, but I really need to get back to work," I said, trying to find a way to politely excuse myself.

Keri's smile faltered for a moment, but she quickly recovered. "Oh, come on, Dan. It's been so long since we've seen each other. Don't you want to hear about my life in New York?"

I couldn't help but roll my eyes at her self-importance. "Actually, Keri, I'm really busy right now. Maybe we can catch up another time?"

My dad looked disappointed, but he didn't push the issue. "Of course, Son. You have a lot on your plate right now. We'll have to plan a family dinner soon, though. It's been too long since we've all been together."

I nodded, grateful for the escape. "Yeah, that sounds great. I'll talk to you soon, Dad."

As I left the restaurant, I couldn't help but think about Emily and what had happened between us. My heart felt heavy, but I knew I had to stay focused on work and moving on. Keri may have been a distraction, but she was the last thing I needed right now.

25

EMILY

I got up and dressed, already dreading the day. I regretted telling my mother about the baby the instant I said it, but seeing her dressed and ready with her purse and keys out when I came out of my room for breakfast a little after nine just crushed me. She was serious about forcing me into an abortion. I let my shoulders fall and picked up a banana from the fruit basket and opened it.

"I've made the appointment. It is in thirty minutes, so I'm glad you're already dressed. We'll just have a consultation with the doctor today, but we can schedule the official appointment on Monday." Mom's tone was cold and uncaring. I knew she cared about me a great deal, but when it came to this, she seemed like a robot. I wasn't sure if she'd been through something similar with her mother or something, but it was like she was on autopilot.

"Mom, I don't want an abortion." I took a bite of the banana and chewed slowly. Her expression didn't change.

"We'll just have the consultation today. You'll see, Emily. The doctors say it's very easy and painless, so you can just go on with your life like this never happened." Mom stood and picked up her purse and keys. "I'll be waiting in the car."

She walked out, and I lingered in the kitchen. I was frustrated with her, but I knew that ultimately, it was my choice. At the very least, the checkup would be good. I needed prenatal vitamins, and the doctor at the free clinic might be able to recommend someone good for my obstetrician. They might also be able to give me something for my morning sickness too, which had gotten so bad I feared I was losing weight instead of gaining like I was supposed to.

I slid my shoes on, grabbed my wallet, and headed for the car. Mom had it running, listening to an oldies station. We didn't speak the entire way to the clinic, which wasn't even in Bellville. It was two towns over in Troy, the county seat. It sat on the south side of town in a little plaza with a dozen other shops. The door had the words *Women's Clinic* painted on it, but there was no official sign. It appeared rundown, like much of the other buildings on this side of town.

Mom led me into the building, and I found a seat next to a teenager who had headphones on. She wore all black clothing and had dark lipstick. She was alone, unlike me. Some parents didn't care at all. Others cared too much—like my mother. At twenty-five, this was my decision, though it would take the words of the doctor to make it clear to Mom. This young girl beside me looked depressed and alone. I was thankful my mother cared. I just wished she'd give me room to breathe.

We waited for at least twenty minutes, and I wondered if they were this far behind already this morning, how long would I have had to wait if the appointment were in the afternoon? The young girl was taken back before me, then the nurse returned to the door and called my name.

"Emily Kline?"

I looked up at her round face and nodded. As I stood, Mom stood too. "Mom, I don't need you to go with me. I'm an adult."

"Nonsense, dear. I need to speak to the doctor too."

The nurse eyed me, as if waiting for my consent, and I shrugged. "Fine." I followed the nurse through the door down the narrow hallway, and she opened a door.

"In here, dear. Mom, you can sit in the chair. Emily, you can sit on the table. The doc will be right with you." The nurse excused herself, and I climbed up and sat on the table, feet dangling.

The room was cold, but Mom's scowl made it colder. "You didn't actually think you could do this alone, did you? I'm your mother."

"Yes, and I've been going to doctor's appointments alone for years. I don't need a babysitter." I didn't want to be hurtful, but she was seriously overstepping.

"Yes, well this is different, now isn't it?" Her peaked eyebrows frustrated me. There was a point where parenting needed to end, and we had crossed that line a long time ago.

The door creaked open and a tall, handsome man walked in, blue eyes, graying hair. He smiled and shut the door behind him before saying, "Emily? And this is Mom, I assume?" He shook my hand, then my mom's.

"Yes."

The doctor sat and looked at his notes. "I'm Dr. Yates. It says here you're interested in termination of pregnancy?" His eyes scanned the page then looked up at me. "Is that true?"

"Uh, not really. My mom—"

"Yes, it's true." Mom was curt and blunt. She interrupted me, and I scowled.

"No, Doctor. It's not actually true. I realize that I probably need some sort of prenatal care, but I'm not interested in—"

"Emily," Mom snapped, cutting me off again, "listen to the doctor. He knows what's best. You'll see that once this is over, you'll move on with your life and be much happier for it."

The doctor held up his hand, and Mom quieted. "Alright, let's start here. Do you want your mother present for this visit?"

Mom scoffed angrily, and my shoulders drooped. I wanted my mother to be a part of it, yes, but only if she could be supportive. Her being this way, insisting on an abortion, wasn't helping me. No girl wants her mother to control her, least of all an adult with autonomy. I sighed and dropped my head.

"No," I mumbled.

"Mrs. Kline, could you be so kind as to let me speak with Emily alone?" The doctor stood and opened the door, and Mom scoffed again.

"But I'm her mother."

"Mrs. Kline, legally, Emily is an adult, and she alone is allowed to make decisions for her medical care."

I felt the room thicken with tension, but Mom left without saying another word. When the door clicked shut, I felt tears welling up and I slouched, picking at my fingernails.

"Alright, then, Emily. Now we can chat properly. Tell me about this. What's going on in your head?" The doctor sat on his stool again, wheeling it closer to me so I was forced to look up at him.

I cleared my throat and sighed deeply. "I'm pregnant. It's been a huge shock because it wasn't planned. I'm in a sort of awkward relationship with the father, but he doesn't know yet. I'm not sure if he wants kids." I grimaced and continued. "Mom obviously thinks aborting is a good idea. I don't."

"Alright, well it is your choice alone, so keep that in mind. Let me ask you, do you feel you're ready for a child?" He looked at me with compassion, and I shrugged.

"I'm not sure I will ever be ready for that responsibility, but I know for a fact that I'm not getting an abortion. Even if I wasn't ready, I'd choose adoption. I'd never do that. Besides, I feel like no one is ready, that a baby comes along and you just do what you have to do because of love." I pressed my hand to my stomach and knew in my heart that I was doing the right thing.

"Well, it sounds to me like your mind is made up." He smiled.

"Yes, it is. I just hoped you'd get my mom off my back." I chuckled and felt the tension wash out of my body. "I also hoped you could maybe refer me to a good doctor. I actually live in Chicago, but based on how things go with the father when I tell him, I may end up moving back here to Monroe County."

"Of course. Well, let's just get some info down first, and I'll definitely point you toward a few great OB/GYNs." He turned and laid his notepad on the counter, pulling out a pen to scribble some notes. "Your full name is Emily Elizabeth Kline?"

"Yes," I told him. He rambled off several more questions, address, social security number, phone number. Then he looked up at me with a serious expression.

"Father's name?"

"Daniel Jacobs, but that's what I know about him. I don't feel comfortable giving his number out, and I don't have his address memorized. I just know how to get there."

"That's alright. All of this stays private in your file." He jotted down a few more things then asked, "Would you like to have a sonogram this morning? See the little guy growing?"

"What? I can do that?" I asked, feeling my heart swelling.

"Of course, and it's free." He stood and picked up his notes. "I'll send a nurse in shortly. Just sit tight."

It took a while. I waited at least twenty minutes in that cold room, staring at the various posters on the walls of babies in utero and the female reproductive organs. The thought of something that large coming out of my small body frightened me, but I reminded myself that every human on this planet came out of a body in a similar fashion and that I'd be okay, even if my mother chose to disown me after this.

When the nurse came in pushing a wheeled cart with a giant machine on it, I tensed. It had a computer monitor and what looked like an old rotary phone with a curly cord attached to it.

"Hi, Emily, I'm Heather. I'm going to do your sonogram." She plugged the machine in and said, "You'll need to lie down here and lift your shirt up."

I did as she instructed. She took some napkins and tucked them into the waistband of my pants and pulled them lower over the small bulge in my belly that was barely noticeable.

"This will be cold," she said as she squirted some jelly of some sort on my stomach. She used the paddle to maneuver around my stomach at different angles until I heard it—a perfect little heartbeat. I watched the monitor as she showed me the baby's head and spine. His tiny little fingers and toes, and then something strange happened.

The nurse's forehead creased, and she twirled the paddle around my belly again and again. Something was wrong with the heartbeat, and it made my heart race. I felt like it was going too fast, like there was something wrong with the baby, but when Heather got a look of complete shock, I froze.

"Well, Emily, it's too early to find the sex. And it's actually a little early for your belly to be this big. Here's why," she said, angling the monitor at me so I could see it more clearly. There on the screen were two perfectly round circles. I couldn't tell at all what it was, but she grinned at me.

"What is it?" I asked, nervous for her answer.

"It's twins. You're having twins."

"Twins?" I asked, relaxing back onto the table. She mumbled on about their measurements, how soon it would be before I found it if they were identical or fraternal. In fact, she did all the talking the rest of the appointment, and even on the ride home, I was still in shock. I endured Mom's lectures, obsessing over this new revelation. I had a bottle of prenatal vitamins in my hand and a prescription for some pills to help with the nausea too, but now, everything had changed.

If one baby seemed impossible, two definitely were. There was no way I could do this on my own. When we got back to my parents' house, I locked myself in my room and turned my phone on to call Charlotte. I saw I'd missed a few calls from Daniel, but my gut churned just thinking of telling him. I dialed Charlotte instead and waited for it to ring through as I tossed myself across my bed.

"Em, hey, how are your parents?"

"They're fine. Look, Char, I'm freaking out. Mom wants me to have an abortion, and so I went to this pregnancy clinic, and goddammit—" I almost started crying. I wanted these babies more than anything, but now I knew I couldn't do it alone. The idea of telling Daniel and his not wanting them was terrifying to me.

"What? What happened?"

"Char, I'm having twins." I blurted my confession out and let the tears fall. "I can't do this on my own at all. What if Dan hates me?" I sobbed, burying my face in my pillow.

"Oh, God, Em. That's harsh. Your Mom actually said that?"

"Yes, she forced me to go to a pregnancy clinic this morning. And I got to see the babies on a sonogram, and I just feel scared he won't want anything to do with me anymore."

"Calm down, Emily. You have to talk to him before you go all fatalistic on me. Okay? Just come back to Chicago. I'll go with you if you want." Charlotte was always so supportive of me.

"You will?" I asked, whimpering and sniffling.

"Of course I will. Just come home."

She was right. I couldn't get too scared of him rejecting me until I at least attempted to talk to him. And I would have plenty of time to deal with the result of that conversation afterward. Sitting around terrified only doubled my suffering because I was suffering now, and I could be suffering again later. I needed to calm down, go home, and tell him.

26

DANIEL

The scantily clad waitress poured another round of drinks, bending over in front of me on purpose to show me her tits. I was certain Michael had paid her extra to do so, and it annoyed me. I liked a good rack as much as any other man, but right now, I was too upset to even think about it. Emily had blindsided me. Even if Evelyn had spoken out of turn and Emily wasn't really going to sue me, she'd shown me her true feelings by not even returning a single message.

"Look, man, it's Saturday night. You need to get over this." Michael tipped his drink up, downing the contents, and gestured at one of the women dancing near a pole on the bar. Her heels were probably six inches tall. I didn't see how she could even walk in them, let alone dance, but her topless body slithered along the pole, grinding on it with ease.

I turned away, not disgusted, but not interested. "We could have just gone to a bar. Why a strip joint?" I asked, picking up the fresh drink and sipping it. I didn't need to get wasted. I'd just screw one of these dancers and feel even worse about myself. I wasn't the type to be unfaithful, and even though I knew in my heart it was over between me and Emily, I wasn't about to throw myself at a woman until it was official. I had to hear her say the words.

"You really need to get laid. Just jump in and pick one already. There are about a dozen women here who would gladly go home with a billionaire, even if it was just a one-nighter." He waved the sultry waitress back over with her bottle of gin, and she filled his drink. I tried to avoid looking at her. "What do you say, honey? You want to go home with my friend?" Michael was clearly drunk, and she knew it. She rolled her eyes at him and patted his shoulder.

"I think you're asking the wrong woman. Maybe try Vixen up there." She pointed to a redhead wrapped around a pole, legs above her head. She spun slowly, revealing both ass cheeks as the thong she wore rode up her crack.

Michael snickered and winked at the woman before she walked away. "Should I go ask Vixen? I wonder if that's her real name."

"Mike, seriously. I'm about to be sued for sexual harassment. I don't need another woman to join in on the fun." I downed my drink and set the glass down hard on the bar.

"No, you need to loosen up. I'm your lawyer, and I'm telling you to go fuck that woman and get over your assistant." He gestured at the woman called Vixen and cupped his drink in his hand.

"I'm not even a little tempted, buddy." I turned on my seat and stood. "You got a ride home? Because you shouldn't be driving." I waited until he mumbled something about an Uber, then walked toward the doors. The hardest part of this whole thing had been not talking to her. If I could have just asked her if her sister was speaking on her behalf, a lot of this anxiety and anger could have been alleviated. I'd at least know.

But not only was she not speaking with me, but the official stance of the firm was that I was not to speak to her. Which meant if I called her and they found out, I risked their not standing behind me should she actually file a lawsuit. I hated it, because she'd torn my heart out and she needed to know how I felt, but my hands were tied.

I let myself out of the club, finding my driver there waiting for me. I climbed in, and he started driving. I assumed back to my house, but I didn't even care where he went. I just wanted him to get me away from Michael and the insistence that I needed rebound sex to get over Emily. I'd never get over Emily. I had fallen for her hard.

At home, I poured another drink, scotch neat, and made my way up to my room, intent on having a shower and calling it a night. I checked my phone again. Still no messages or missed calls from her. It had been a few days with complete silence, after a few weeks of barely connecting. I didn't even know what to do with myself. I'd typically settle in and watch a show or read a book, but neither of those things appealed to me. Nothing appealed to me right now, not even work. A huge chunk had been carved out of my heart, and nothing would fill it ever again.

I undressed, leaving my clothes in a pile on the bathroom floor as I turned on the water and let the shower steam up the entire room. The hot water nearly scalded my skin, turning me bright pink, but at least I was feeling something. I stood there letting water rush over my body, pressing my head against the cool tile. I closed my eyes and saw her, smiling at me as she knelt on my office floor mopping up the coffee mess.

I should have restrained myself, followed Michael and Grace's suggestion to keep my mind focused. Why hadn't I listened to them? What was so mesmerizing about Emily that I had completely ignored their suggestions and dived into a messy affair? Could I even call that a relationship now, when I knew that Emily had only intended to bait me and come after my reputation and money?

I growled at my own stupidity and pushed off the tile. I washed my face, soap getting in my eyes and stinging, but even that wasn't as painful as what she did to me. I believed her fully, trusted her, but if Evelyn was telling me the truth—and I believed she was–then Emily had just been putting on an act. So, why was I here in this shower feeling like touching myself just thinking of her? Did I have a desire for pain, a need to be punished for my stupidity?

I shut the water off, realizing if I stayed there a second longer, I'd be masturbating to thoughts of her. That would only make losing her more painful. I climbed out and dried off, dressing in some boxers and a T-shirt. Then I poured myself another drink from the bottle on my nightstand and climbed into bed after downing it. I just wanted to sleep. The whiskey helped, pulling me into dreamland almost immediately.

... Emily leans over me, whispering me awake. She smells like whiskey, scotch maybe, or a flavored bourbon aged in an old barrel. Her smile is intoxicating. I feel myself growing hard just thinking of her lips touching me. I open my eyes to see her straddling me, the sheets falling off her body revealing her perfect curves. She runs her hands through my hair and down my chest, teasing me with her touch. I can feel her hot breath on my neck as she whispers in my ear, "I want you."

I don't need to be asked twice. I flip her over so that I'm on top, pinning her down with my arms. Our lips meet in a fiery passion, our tongues dancing together in sync. I can feel her body shudder beneath me as I slide my hand between her legs, feeling how wet she is for me.

I start to kiss down her neck, my lips trailing down to her breasts. I take one nipple into my mouth, swirling my tongue around it while I use my hand to play with the other. Emily moans loudly, arching her back as she grinds against me.

I can feel myself losing control, my own desire taking over. I want to taste her.

I slowly slide her panties off her and slowly pull her legs apart. She shudders as she feels the cool air on her exposed treasure. I can feel her shaking with anticipation and drive my tongue deep inside her, tasting her inner sweetness. She cries out and holds my head against her as she writhes beneath me. I push her legs apart and slide my head up and down her slit, teasing her with my tongue.

"Is this what you want?" I ask, slowing my pace.

"Just give it to me," she moans. Her voice is so clear, so arousing it makes my dick throb. I want her.

I move my head faster and more urgently, pushing her closer and closer to the edge of pleasure. Her moans are louder and more passionate as I move my tongue around her clit, sending waves of pleasure through her body. I feel her fingers grip onto my hair, pulling me deeper into her. Her moans are loud and deep. She holds my head to her, encouraging me to keep lapping at her, to keep her on the edge.

My lips greedily kiss the skin of her inner thighs. I smell the sweet scent of her perfume and feel the silkiness of her skin. I taste the saltiness of her cum on her folds and feel the goosebumps form on her skin as I suck her. My hands feel the softness of her body. I see her look down at me as I look up at her.

Emily is spread out on the bed, her hands gripping the sheets as she spreads her legs. Her legs are shaking, her breath coming in gasps. Her breasts are heaving, her nipples hard and erect. She lies there with her eyes closed, head tilted back and mouth parted. Her chest rises and falls with each breath. Her breasts bob slightly with each inhale. Her body is flushed, her skin red and hot as orgasm washes over her in waves. Then I position myself between her knees.

I slide my tip inside her, feeling her gasp with pleasure from the sensation. I grab her by the wrists and push her arms above her head, holding them in place as I grind against her. Her breathing quickens, and I feel her arching her back, pushing her hips up to meet mine. She gasps at the sudden sensation of pleasure that radiates through us both.

I start to thrust deep within her, feeling every inch of her tightness surround me. Emily wraps her legs around me as she cries out in delight at the intense sensations coursing through both of us.

We move in unison as our bodies become one, dancing together in a rhythm that only we could understand. She screams out my name as she reaches her peak, and I can't help but join in on the chorus of pleasure. "Oh, God!" we both moan out together as we reach our climaxes in perfect harmony....

I woke, my body already plunging into climax, and I threw the covers back. It had been years since I'd had a wet dream, and damned if I didn't have to rush for the toilet gripping my cock as hard as I could to stop the mess from spraying out all over the carpet. My heart pounded as I released, letting the cum drain from my hard dick as I gently stroked it. I leaned one arm on the wall behind the toilet and clenched my eyes shut.

Even in my sleep, I wanted her. How could I let this happen to me?

27

EMILY

Charlotte carried my suitcase for me, lugging it up the few flights of stairs to my apartment. After bickering with my mother all day Sunday, I'd booked a flight home for Monday afternoon. It was early evening now and I was spent. I slumped onto my old, worn couch, curling into myself without a thought about dinner, or unpacking, or even something to drink. Charlotte perched carefully on the edge of the coffee table and rested her hand on my knee. I told her on the drive from the airport home how Mom had reacted, and she was sympathetic.

"I can't imagine how you feel. Even after your mom found out you weren't interested in an abortion, she kept pushing you?" Her thumb rubbed back and forth across my jeans, and I pulled my leg away.

"Yeah, she thinks I'm throwing my life away. I don't think so."

Charlotte frowned and moved to the couch beside me, sinking in on the broken cushion. She mimicked my position, hugging her knees to her chest. Her hair fell around her face in a mess, unbrushed but still gorgeous. I wondered if Daniel would still think I was pretty when he saw my stomach starting to bulge, and I had to turn away from her. Everything made me think of him, probably because I had inadvertently put a distance between us that should never have been there. I should have told him from the beginning.

"I don't think you're throwing your life away. I think your life is going to look different from how she wanted it to, maybe even different from how you wanted it to, but it's not thrown away. You're just taking a different path. That's all."

I forced a weak smile and took a cleansing breath. Char always had a way of seeing the positive side of things. I'd been trying to do the same thing, thinking about the positives. I was already in love with these two little lives growing inside me. My life was already different from how I had planned it to be, but that hadn't changed when I found out I was pregnant. That had changed the moment Daniel took an interest in me. I'd never in a million years thought I'd meet someone so amazing.

"You really love him, don't you?"

"I do..." I mumbled, tucking my chin to my chest. "And it's not because I'm pregnant. I have known I was in love for a long time."

"You need to tell him, Em. He deserves to know. He's probably wondering why you haven't called or texted him." I looked up at her expression—concerned and caring.

"I know. I've just felt guilty about hiding this from him, and afraid that he'd think I was lying to him. He said the one thing that would tear us apart was a lie. I've been hiding this for so long now that I'm starting to show. Granted, I'm showing much earlier than a normal pregnancy because it's twins, but still. He'll think—"

"It doesn't matter what he thinks, as long as you tell him. Okay?"

My stomach gurgled, and I felt ill. The anti-nausea meds were buried in my suitcase, and I hadn't eaten, so morning sickness was about to kick my ass. I tried to swallow the bile that rose in the back of my throat, but it was a losing battle. This was a part of pregnancy I hated, throwing up all the time. I stood and walked to my suitcase, unzipping it, and as I did, I heard keys jingle in the lock. I froze. The only person who had keys to my apartment other than me was Evelyn, and I didn't want to see her right now.

The door swung open and she burst in. She had wide eyes and a judgmental expression as she shut the door and stared down at me rifling through my suitcase in search of my medicine. "What do you want, Eve?"

"I can't believe you didn't tell me you were pregnant."

My shoulders slumped. I found the medicine and pulled the bottle out, twisting the childproof cap fruitlessly. My body tensed, a few hiccups escaping before a burp. It was coming up already. No time for medicine. I bolted to my feet and started for the bathroom, but it was too late. I threw up all over the carpet, my sweatshirt, my jeans, and the torn linoleum in the hallway.

By the time I got to the toilet, I had nothing left in me but sobs. I hated my family, talking about me behind my back as if they were better than me or could control my life with their gossip. It was how small-town life went. It was the reason I wanted out of Monroe County. I wanted to be invisible, to disappear into the masses where no one knew me and I could just live my life my way. I should never have gone home to visit.

Charlotte was there, holding my hair back as I sobbed and blew my nose. Evelyn was there too, arms folded, staring at me emotionlessly. Char helped me clean up and pull my soiled sweatshirt off, and I pushed past Evelyn and headed for my bedroom. Eve followed, heels clicking on the floor.

"Char, I need to speak to my sister alone."

Charlotte lingered, waiting for me to dismiss her, and I waved my hand. Evelyn would be cruel to me. I knew that much. Char didn't need to be around for that. "I'll clean up the floor, okay?" Her compassion warmed my heart.

She left, and I peeled off my nasty jeans, kicking my shoes off by my dresser. Evelyn watched me change, shaking her head at my changing body. "Mom told me, but I didn't believe it. And you're far enough along that you're showing? What, did you have sex with him on your first day?"

"Can you lay off, Eve? This is hard enough without you judging me." I pulled open my dresser drawer and tried to find some leggings. Most of my pants would be too tight now, anyway. I needed to invest in some maternity clothing soon.

"Look, I don't necessarily agree with Mom. After having a kid, I know what it does to you." Her voice softened as she leaned on the door frame. "I wouldn't abort either. I just think you're in for a world of pain now. He's never going to support you. You're just going to be the fat assistant who got pregnant now. He'll find a new woman to bone and forget about you."

Her words stung. I didn't want to believe that. Daniel loved me. I knew he did. And I loved him. My mind was at war with itself, trying to decide what was true. I pulled a T-shirt on and found some yoga pants. Evelyn continued telling me how badly I messed up as I sat on the edge of my bed and forced my legs into the pants. The ceaseless lectures were pounding my self-confidence into the dirt.

"What if he accepts the baby, Eve? What if he wants to get married and he's really in love with me?" My question made her grow quiet. She studied my face, her expression changing. I saw hatred, then sympathy, then anger, then compassion. She walked over and sat next to me.

"Marrying a man because you're pregnant with his child is not a good idea. You know how many women have done that and regretted it?" She wrung her hands in her lap and continued. "Emily, I'm trying to stick up for you, help you. You know? You can't marry this guy. He never cared about you. If he had, he'd have called to find out where you were… what you were doing. He hasn't even called once, has he?" Her eyes bored into me, slicing through my soul. Her words were not a genuine question, but an accusation, and a correct one at that.

"No, he hasn't," I replied, chin down.

"Can't you see? Mom might have her own ways of trying to take care of you, and I admit she's a little over the top sometimes, but we both care. Me and Mom. I think you should come live with me for a while. We'll clear out the baby's room and you can bring your bed. It will be good for you. You won't have to stay with Mom and Dad. You can find a job here in the city that fits your degree better. Please, say you will?"

My stomach rolled again, and I shook my head. "No, Eve. I have to do this my way. Okay? I am going to show everyone that no matter how difficult it is, I made my bed and I will lie in it. I'm not going to mooch off anyone. I'm going to be my own person."

I smoothed my hands down the front of my yoga pants and stood. "I think I need to eat something or I'm going to throw up again."

Evelyn stood in a huff, angry with me for refusing her invitation. "Alright, well don't say I didn't warn you. It's going to be impossible."

She led the way to the living room that still smelled like vomit, but Charlotte had gotten the mess mostly cleaned up. Evelyn stormed to the door and opened it, turning back over her shoulder to say, "I think you're making a mistake." When she left, she slammed the door behind herself. I stared at the wet floor, soggy from Char's attempt to clean.

"I'm sorry she's like that, Em." Charlotte dropped the rag into the bucket of water she was using to clean the carpet and picked up my pills from the spot on the floor where I'd dropped them. "Take one and eat something."

"Char, I'm a wreck. I can't eat. I can't sleep. I am so upset. I feel like Daniel will never speak to me again, and it's not that I don't want to do this by myself. I can. I just want a family—my family. I want him." More tears came, and I didn't stop them.

"Then call him," she said. "Tell him. Just get this over with so you can feel better."

She was right. Ripping the bandage off was the only way now. I sat down at the kitchen table and took my phone out of my purse, dropped on the table as I walked in. I opened my contacts and found Daniel's name and pressed call. The phone rang several times and went to voicemail, but I didn't want to leave a message. I wanted to hear his voice, so I called again. This time, it went straight to voice-mail, no ringing. He had shut his phone off.

The only thing worse than not knowing was knowing that it was not good. He'd never have turned his phone off like that if he wanted to speak to me. The only thing I could think was that he was upset with me for not calling all weekend. He had every right to be upset with me. I didn't leave a message either, because all I could do was cry now, and I didn't want him to hear me crying. I put my phone back in my purse and folded my arms on the table, collapsing over them.

I felt hopeless. I couldn't do this without him.

28

DANIEL

My phone vibrated in my pocket, and I didn't even bother looking at it. I just reached in and held the power button down until I felt the double vibration in rapid succession indicating it was powering down. Michael and I hovered over the paperwork for our biggest banking client. Their attempts to build a new office building for their corporate office move to West Loop was being held up in zoning and they weren't happy. As their lawyers, it was our duty to push things like this along, but it was frustrating the hell out of me in particular—especially given it was a Sunday afternoon and I was in the office instead of sitting by my pool sipping lemonade.

"The damn zoning board didn't approve the application. They said it didn't arrive by the deadline for this month's zoning committee." Michael rifled through a few of the papers scattered on the conference room table and folded the map back to look. He found the application which I'd had Emily file weeks ago. The time stamp on the document, done downstairs with the notary, indicated it was completed on time. I pointed to that time stamp.

"Look..." I shook my head. "Was it Cheryl? Is she the one who told you this? Because I've had trouble with her before." I sank into the chair behind me and rubbed my forehead. "You'll have to call the board first thing in the morning to iron this out. The papers were faxed in on time."

Michael stacked the forms up into a single pile and grumbled a bit. I knew Emily had done a fantastic job on these, though he wanted to pin the screw-up on her. I checked her work every single day to ensure it was being done well. She hadn't made a single mistake, at least not where her work was concerned.

"Well, I think we need to check the fax records, anyway." He folded the map and stacked it with the other papers, then shoved them all in his briefcase. "Because there is a chance that you signed off on the paperwork, but she never did the faxes."

"Olivia does the faxes, not Emily," I snapped, scowling at him. He really had it in for her, and it aggravated me. "I wish you would let up a little."

Now that we'd been over every file, I pulled my phone from my pocket and turned it back on. Michael locked his briefcase and set it on the floor, but he stood there and shoved his hand in his pocket, staring down at me with distaste. "Dan, you don't really have room to talk. You thought she was so amazing until she up and filed a lawsuit on you."

"She didn't file a lawsuit. Her sister threatened one. Get that part straight. And her work has been impeccable, stellar even. She's the best assistant I've had." My phone vibrated as notifications of more missed calls came in, though I didn't check them yet. I was too upset with him.

"Well, come tomorrow morning, we're letting her go. We have a very straightforward reason—she hasn't shown up for work in days. You got a half-assed excuse from Olivia about her being sick, and then you got an email stating she'd be out of town." Michael's head shook like a bobblehead dog on the dashboard of an old Volkswagen van. I wanted to smack him, but I knew he was right. She had missed quite a lot of work and had no real excuse for the absenteeism.

It didn't feel right, though, firing her for this. She hadn't filed a suit, and for all I knew, her sister had only made threats. Emily had been down for weeks, depression, maybe. I'd seen her apartment, the conditions she lived in. She needed this job.

"What if we move her? Make her Grace's personal assistant instead of mine? I can take a few weeks off work, work from home. Let Emily adjust to somewhere else." The very fact that I was still pleading for her job should have revealed to him that I had feelings for her. It cut me to my core to think that she'd be on her own in this huge city, fending for herself. It didn't matter that she'd played me. Love was blind, and I guess so was I.

"I can't believe you still stand up for her, Dan. She got you to sleep with her and she's threatening a lawsuit because of that. She hasn't attempted contact with you for days, right after the suit was threatened, and you still care." He sighed and shook his head again. "You really are a glutton for punishment."

"It's called love, Mike, and if you ever loved someone the way I loved Emily, you'd understand." I looked down at my phone, needing a distraction. The notifications were from Emily. Two missed calls, zero voicemails. My heart sank. She had tried to call me and I'd ignored it. Michael would tell me to ignore her anyway, but I'd done it inadvertently. If she had called, I'd have answered, and this argument would be about something different.

"Look, I get it. You care about her, which is why Grace and I are going to chip in out of our profit sharing to get her a nice severance package. It should keep her going for six months while she finds a new job. Alright? But you can't just let someone who threatened to sue continue working here."

He picked up his case and rubbed the back of his neck. "I'm sorry for causing such a stir. I just care about you as a friend, and I care about this firm. A lawsuit like that won't sink us, but the media circus around it just might. I don't want to see you go through that, or the firm you've built. And I also don't want my reputation tarnished with the fallout either. Neither does Grace. Just let us handle this, and swear to me you won't make contact with her until she's terminated."

I hated it, the way he thought he could handle me—because that's what he was doing. He wasn't managing a situation, he was controlling me, micromanaging my actions and reactions to mitigate damage.

"Yeah, I swear. Okay? I know how this works." My mouth said the words, but my heart screamed to ignore him. I knew he was right, though. Any court in the world would see my response to Evelyn's threats against me and the firm as hostile. Even if Emily called me again, I needed to ignore it.

I waited a full twenty minutes after Michael left before making my way downstairs. I didn't want the uncomfortable conversation to continue in the elevator or on the street while waiting for my driver. I had a hard enough time clearing the notifications and pretending my heart didn't really want to call Emily and clear this whole thing up. She didn't know it, but I loved her enough that if money was what she wanted, I'd give it all to her. I just wanted her too, not just a settlement.

I stepped off the elevator and headed out the front door, locking up behind me, and when I turned to walk toward the car, I saw Evelyn standing there. The glare on her face, coupled with the way she stood with arms over her chest, told me she was angry again. At least I knew who she was this time as I walked into the confrontation.

"Mr. Jacobs, I think you remember who I am." Her nose seemed pointier than it did last week, or maybe I was confusing her with the Wicked Witch from that old movie.

"Yes, I know who you are," I said, walking past her toward my car. That face had been burned into my conscience. I didn't think I'd ever forget it or get it out of my nightmares.

"Listen, buddy—"

"Look, if you're going to file a lawsuit, just get it over with. Okay?" I spun around, still several strides from the car. I heard the driver's door shut and knew he'd be opening the door for me.

She scoffed, snarling her lip up like a rabid dog ready to attack. "Tell me, when you hired Emily, did you think about how you'd fuck up her life before you did it? What about when you screwed her in your office? Did you plan to knock her up and then dump her in the ditch when you were done with her?" She gestured with her hands as she spoke, but I wasn't intimidated. I still clung to the hope that she was speaking out of turn. My heart had to believe that this was not what Emily was like.

"Have you even spoken to her? Has she put you up to this?" I took a few steps forward, but my conscience told me to stop. Acting in an aggressive or threatening manner would only make things worse.

"Didn't you hear me?" she asked, ignoring my question. "Emily is pregnant. You knocked her up, and now she's pissed and thinking about getting rid of it." Evelyn's nostrils flared as she moved closer to me, clearly not afraid of me.

So many thoughts raced through my mind. "You're lying." I clenched my jaw and shook my head. "If she was pregnant, I'd have been the first person she told." It made sense, the sickness, calling into work, being overly emotional. But she'd have told me.

"I'm not lying. She went home to visit my parents, and my mother took her to an abortion clinic… So you're right. Maybe she's not pregnant anymore. But either way, you are going to cough up money to help her. Because she's refusing to let her family help her, and I for one won't stand by and watch her fail."

Her words fell on deaf ears. I turned to my car and tried to stop the rage boiling in my chest. I heard Evelyn following me. The driver grimaced at me and stood aside as I neared, and Evelyn grabbed my arm and tried to get me to turn around. I yanked my arm out of her grasp and whipped around, leaning over her. She wasn't as short as Emily, but I still towered over her small frame.

"You need to back off. And you need to listen to me carefully. I have enough power and resources to bury you, your sister, your parents, and their business so deep, they'll never dig out. Do you understand me? And my firm is one of the most powerful in this city, hell, even the country. You'll find yourself so swamped in litigation, it will cost you everything and I'll still win."

I turned and climbed into the car before she could respond. The driver shut the door, and I locked it while he attempted to get Evelyn to step away. She was so angry, even after he climbed in, that she was pounding on the window and screaming slurs at me which I could only just barely hear thanks to the soundproof glass. As angry as she was, I had to believe part or all of her story could be true. If it were my sister and I believed she was being played, I'd be furious too.

But I knew Emily, or at least I thought I did. She'd have told me if she was pregnant. That only made me more confused and frustrated. I was glad I hadn't answered the phone during that meeting. After that display, I could only imagine how that conversation would have gone if Emily really was going to sue me. And it all would have played out right in front of Michael.

"Are you alright, sir?" the driver asked after rolling down the window that separated us.

"Fine, thank you. I appreciate your taking the lead there at the end." I felt my phone buzz again, and for a split second, I hoped it was Emily.

"You're welcome, sir. Just going home now?" he asked, glancing in the mirror.

"Yeah, home..." I pulled my phone out to see a text from Michael reminding me of a meeting first thing in the morning. It was not the message I hoped to receive.

I laid my head on the headrest and closed my eyes, listening to the sound of the window going back up. This was too overwhelming. I wanted to wake up and find it was all just one big nightmare. Except, if that were true, then every single second I'd spent with Emily would have been part of that nightmare, the intimate moments, the love I felt. And how could that be true? How could love be such a cruel and twisted figment of my imagination?

29

EMILY

I was nervous as I dressed for work. My skirts were all just slightly too tight, which made them snug across my hips. I knew Olivia would judge me, but I had no choice. Until I found some maternity clothes, I had to make do with outfits that were too tight. It wasn't any tighter than a pair of skinny jeans, but it wasn't exactly professional, either. I checked myself out in the mirror. The extra snugness accentuated the curve of my ass. I thought it was sexy, but sexy wasn't how I was supposed to look at work.

Instead of the jacket that went with my suit, I chose a sweater that hung low, covering most of my backside. It was a bit warm for a sweater, but it would be better than hearing the lecture. It also was a bit loose around the middle, which would hide the tiny bulge I had. Though, I did stand and look in the mirror as I pulled the outfit tight against my stomach to see how my body was changing. The nurse at the clinic was right. I was well on my way to showing quite early.

Shaking the sweater out so it hung loosely again, I put on some earrings, a touch of makeup, and picked up my purse. With a new routine of regular tiny meals and the addition of the anti-nausea medicine, I felt well enough to work. I also felt badly for missing so many days, and I was ready to jump back in the saddle and catch up on any missed assignments Daniel had for me.

I was eager to speak with him too, maybe over lunch, and discuss exactly why I had been absent. He hadn't called or texted me, which made me think he was very upset, but I knew when I told him what was going on, he'd understand why I hadn't been at work. I just hoped that he'd also be happy about the babies and not angry with me for delaying telling him. And as for the bit about his not seeing himself as a father, well, he'd have to get over that. Like it or not, he was going to be a father. Even if he didn't want a relationship with me.

The subway was packed, standing room only, and my feet hurt already from the walk to the station. I wished I was really showing. Maybe one of the men seated around me would give up his seat, but no one did. So I stood, clinging to the pole in the center of the aisle as the train took me to my station. I arrived early, no rushing to the building, so I stopped and got Daniel his favorite blend of coffee and one for myself as well. I smiled as I thought about seeing him again. God, I'd missed him.

But when the elevator doors slid open and I saw Grace and Michael standing near reception, I knew something was off. They were always locked in their offices hard at work, or not even in for the day when I arrived. They straightened, ended their hushed conversation, and turned to face me as I stepped off the elevator. Fear trickled down my spine as Grace spoke.

"Ms. Kline, we'd like to speak to you for a moment." She used a very professional voice, hands folded in front of her waist.

"Uh... sure," I said, glancing between her face and Michael's. Jill was there instantly, taking Daniel's coffee from my hand. It had his name written on it, so it was obvious where it went.

"I'll take this in for you," she said, grimacing and offering a look of compassion. When she walked away, I addressed Michael.

"What is it, sir?" My hand trembled, coffee sloshing, and I grasped both hands around the paper cup.

"Emily, while we both agree that your work here has been done well and you've made very few mistakes, your conduct has been very unprofessional. Unbecoming, even." Michael's voice sounded robotic, monotone. He had no emotion on his face, not even a furrowed brow. "We have decided to terminate you effective immediately. Jill has taken the liberty of cleaning out your desk for you."

Grace rounded the end of the reception desk and picked up a box and carried it over to me. The few things I had in my desk were all in this box. I stared into it as I accepted it from her in shock. "What?"

"Ms. Kline," Grace said sternly, "it came to our knowledge that your family has threatened a lawsuit against the firm and against Mr. Jacobs. While we cannot prevent you or your family from pursuing any legal action you may feel is warranted, given Mr. Jacobs's interaction with you in the privacy of his office, we do strongly recommend that you reconsider litigation. It will not end well for you."

"Because we do respect your financial situation," Michael cut in, "we are prepared to offer six months' salary in addition to your final weekly compensation check. We hope this affords you plenty of time to arrange a new job. And Olivia will write you a professional letter of recommendation."

I felt dizzy. I blinked my eyes as they faded from light to dark, my vision blurring. My blood pressure had to be skyrocketing. "My family did what?" I mumbled. "I have to see Dan."

"I'm sorry, Ms. Kline, but contact with Mr. Jacobs is off limits now. You may not speak to him, and it is strongly recommended that you do not try to call him, email, or send text messages. Any attempt on your part to communicate with him will be considered hostile, and we will be forced to defend him."

"But I—"

"I'm sure you may be confused, but we take threats seriously. If you need further information as to the nature of this threat, you should speak with your sister, Evelyn." Grace was cold, her tone exacting.

I blinked slowly and looked up at her face. I had no idea what she was talking about, but I didn't put it past Evelyn to do something like this. I felt like I was going to pass out, my head swimming. "Please, I think this is a big misunderstanding. I need to speak with Daniel."

"Mr. Jacobs is in a meeting. You are not to speak to him or try to contact him." Michael reached into his pocket and pulled out a crisp sheet of paper folded in thirds. He dropped it in the box and continued. "This is a restraining order, filed last week against you. If you attempt to make contact with him, set foot on his property or that of the firm, you can be prosecuted to the fullest extent of the law."

I knew they didn't like me, but they were taking this a bit too far. "Guys, I swear, this is just a misunderstanding." I felt tears brimming in my eyes and had the urge to drop the box and rush past them. I needed to see Dan.

Michael turned his back and walked off, and Grace put her hands out and herded me back into the elevator, which was being held open by Olivia, whom I hadn't even seen walk up. "I understand this is difficult, Emily, but please, we are trying to protect Dan." Olivia talked in comforting tones. I blinked and tears streamed down my cheeks. "Please just respect him at this time, alright? I'm sure eventually, things will calm down and he will be open to hearing from you."

The doors slid shut, obscuring my view, and the elevator descended. What the hell just happened? I stood there sobbing as the doors opened to a different floor, and the people ready to join me stood back, staring. They didn't get in the elevator, and I was relieved. I rode the thing to the ground floor and found a bench outside the building to sit down on. When he hadn't contacted me, I assumed he was upset, but I never thought this would be his response. He didn't even know I was pregnant yet, and how would I tell him now? They would file a suit against me? For telling him I was having his baby?

The thought made me cry harder. I was so angry I pulled out my phone and dialed Evelyn's number. Her voice was groggy when she answered, like I had awakened her, but I didn't care.

"Em? It's early. What's wrong?"

"Goddammit, Eve! What the hell have you done? You told Daniel I was going to sue him? Do you even know what is happening? I'm fired. I have no job now, thanks to you. I'm fucking pregnant, and I have no job."

A few people passing by stared at me, and when I glared at them they looked away. I was thankful I didn't know any of them, that they walked right past the law building and didn't enter. It didn't matter that I was sitting on a bench in public, raging at my sister. No one in this town knew me, and I had nothing to lose.

"Em, I—"

"I hate you, Evelyn. Okay? You have no idea what you've done. I needed him. I love him. I can't do this without him." I cried so hard I thought I'd throw up. I didn't want a severance package. I wanted a family.

"Emily, please. Stop this. You come stay with me. I'll take care of you."

"You think I'd even consider that? You ruined my life. I never told you to go talk to him. You had no right to even say a word to him, and you told him I was going to sue. For what? Everything we did was consensual. I wanted it as much as he did."

"He was using you." Evelyn's voice grew hostile. She didn't care about me. She just wanted to be right. She couldn't stand that I could find love with someone powerful and wealthy, and she was jealous.

"You can't use someone who wants what you're asking. That's not abuse." I hung up, too angry to continue talking to her. I'd say something I'd regret later on.

The box wasn't heavy, but my feet still hurt. I limped to the station, found the first train headed the right way, and slumped into a seat. An elderly man on the train a few rows away from me pulled a handkerchief out and handed it to me without a word. I took it and sobbed, blowing my nose hard in the small, thin cloth. It was something Dan would have done for me, or for any woman. He was kind like that.

That only made me cry harder.

This was why he hadn't responded to me or answered. He'd seen how I lived, my apartment, how poor I was, and he'd decided to cut me off. Only he didn't even have the guts to cut me off himself. He had to have his staff do it for him. And the worst part was, he told me the only thing that would end our relationship was a lie, but I hadn't lied. Unless Evelyn had told him I was pregnant too, which meant he knew and that was why he'd ended things.

My head hurt. My heart hurt. I wanted to go to sleep and not wake up for months, until my heart healed. This couldn't have been Daniel's doing. He'd never treat me like this. Or maybe that was just an imagination I'd had of him and Evelyn had actually been right. If he were the sexist bigot Evelyn told me he was, this was exactly how he'd act, and I'd just gone off on her.

I was so confused, so overwhelmed. My mind rehearsed a million things I'd say to him if he called me. I replayed every conversation we'd had over the past few weeks in my head, trying to make sense of things, but nothing made sense.

By the time I got home, I was a complete wreck. The handkerchief donated to my sob-fest was soaked in snot and tears. I threw it away and left the box of my things on the counter before stripping off and climbing into bed in just my bra and panties.

Why hadn't I told him immediately when I found out? Why had I been so scared of his knowing I was pregnant? Now that I had the confidence to tell him, it was too late. He didn't want me. Maybe he never wanted me for anything other than an easy lay, and I had been so easy. I never even played hard to get. I cradled my stomach and let the tears and wails of anger and pain pour out of me. What on earth would I do now?

30

DANIEL

"Sir, your coffee?" Jill's head popped into my office unannounced. I knew the moment I saw her that something wasn't kosher. The worry lines on her forehead told a story of stress and conflict. I looked up and furrowed my brow, restraining the urge to snap at her for entering my office without being called upon.

"What's wrong?" I asked her as she tiptoed across the carpet and set the coffee down. She never entered my office without knocking.

"I, uh… Just bringing your morning brew," she said, forcing a smile.

"Jill, don't mess with me. You never just walk in here. What's going on?" I rose, straightening my tie. My gut clenched, and I had a suspicion that Emily was part of whatever it was that was going on.

"Sir, I just…" She sighed. "I have to go back to my desk. I'm sure Michael will explain in a moment."

I wanted to rush out to the foyer and find out what was happening, but before Jill even made her exit, Michael walked in and held his hand up. I had already rounded the end of my desk, ready to follow Jill out as she exited. Michael's hand pressed into my chest and he shut the door behind Jill.

"Calm down, Dan." He gently nudged me backward, and I clenched my fists. "It's done."

"What's done?" I asked. I tried to sidestep past him, but he stepped with me.

"Emily is gone. Terminated, with a very nice parting gift." I watched him flip the lock on the door, and then he pressed both hands to my chest as if to calm me.

"Mike, I need to speak with her."

"No, you aren't doing that." He was firm, pushing back as I stepped forward. "This went too far the entire time. Even if it was just a threat, she was horrible for your reputation. I've taken the steps necessary to protect you even if you won't protect yourself."

"You've done what?" I pushed back. "What did you do?" I knew they planned to terminate her, but I hadn't given approval. Human resources knew better than to do anything without my consent.

"She is gone, Daniel, and you need to let it go. We filed a restraining order on her. She won't be in contact with you, and you can move on with your life now."

Michael stood between me and the door, and all I could think was that if he wouldn't get out of my way, I'd make him. I balled up my fist and drew back, taking a swing at him. He dodged the swing, hooking me around my gut, and pushed me backward until I slammed onto the couch and smacked my head on the wall.

"Dammit, Michael," I shouted, pushing myself back up. He held his hands out as I balled my fists again, but this time, he didn't stop me as I advanced toward the door. "You had no right." I swung the door open and burst into the hallway, already reaching for my phone to call my driver if necessary.

"Dan, stop!" he yelled, chasing after me. "Dan, as partner in this firm, I have a right to hire and fire as I see fit."

I stopped abruptly and turned on my heel to glare at him. "Yeah? So do I. And you're next on that list, so keep talking." My chest heaved, and he glared at me. We'd been through a lot of things together, and this would be a shitty way to dissolve our partnership, but be that as it may, he was just a cog in the wheel. Emily wasn't. She was everything to me, and it took almost losing her to know that. "I don't care if she sues me. I'll pay it. I don't care if the firm goes under. I'll file bankruptcy. I'll start over somewhere."

"Dan, you can't mean that." Now his voice was calm. He was getting the point. She was my everything, and he sent her away like a common whore.

"I do. And if you want to take the firm and the clients, you can fucking have them. I love her, and I'm going after her. If you try to stop me, I'll fire you and Grace, and anyone else who tries to get in my way."

"Dan, please."

"I mean it, Michael. Back off."

I punched the elevator button, hoping she hadn't gotten too far, but it took too long. I couldn't stand there waiting. I had to do something. I darted to the emergency exit near the stairwell and raced down. My feet couldn't go fast enough, and sending a message to my driver while I ran, I nearly fell a few times, catching myself on the banister, but it didn't slow my progress. I slammed the door open on the ground floor and rushed out to the sidewalk, but it was empty. No sign of her.

I only had to wait a few seconds for my driver to pull up. I climbed in quickly, barking out, "Emily's place. Now. You remember, right?"

"Yes, Mr. Jacobs," he said calmly and pulled into traffic. The midmorning rush was worse than normal. If it were me behind the wheel, I'd have laid on my horn a billion times. My foot pressed into the carpet beneath it, unconsciously imagining pressing the gas pedal. I needed to get there faster. If traffic would just clear, I could beat her home. Or maybe she wasn't going home, but I had a good feeling that she was.

When the car was only a few blocks away, still only rolling a few miles an hour, I snapped, "Stop. I'll walk."

The driver obediently stopped the car, and I climbed out, running as fast as I could the last few blocks. I must have looked strange running through the worst neighborhood in Chicago dressed in an Armani suit, but I didn't care. The only thing on my mind was getting to her, convincing her that Michael didn't speak for me. That he didn't know what I wanted. I had to know if what Evelyn said was true. Why would Emily come to work if she planned to sue me? Why had Grace and Michael not thought of that? This was all just some huge miscommunication.

The elevator was waiting on me when I entered her building. I pressed the button for her floor repeatedly until the doors shut and it began its ascent. It stopped at every floor, worsening my agony. I paced the tiny space like a lion in a cage. There was so much emotion pent up in my chest, I thought my heart would explode.

The second the doors opened, I ran to her door and pounded. "Emily! Open the door." I pounded so hard my hand hurt. Emily's neighbor popped her head out the door and watched me. "Emily, please open up."

There was no response from the other side, not a sound. I turned to the neighbor who was staring. "Is she home? Did she come home a bit ago?"

The woman nodded. "Yeah. I heard her crying." She jerked her chin upward. "Is she crying over you?" the woman asked, looking at me as if I were a snake in the grass.

"Yes..." I turned back to the door and pounded harder. "Emily, please, it's Dan. I know you're home. Let me explain."

I felt my own eyes welling up at the thought that she was refusing to open the door. I was about to start shouting my apologies and questions when the door opened a crack. The chain was on. All I could see was one eye, and the mascara streaking down her cheek.

"Emily, please let me in. There has been a huge misunderstanding."

"I don't know, Dan..." Her voice was small, timid.

"Please," I begged, praying she'd give me a chance.

The door shut. I heard the chain being removed, then the door opened again. Emily stood there with a bathrobe on, hanging open in front. She wore only a bra and panties. Her creamy skin... God, I missed that. And her stomach bulged just above the waistband of her panties. So it was true.

She caught me looking at her stomach as she shut the door, and tears cascaded down her cheeks.

"I'm sorry I didn't tell you. I'm sorry that Evelyn did what she did. I'm sorry that you had to see me like this, that I hurt you so badly that you had me fired. Dan, I'm sorry. I—"

I gripped her face in my hands and covered her mouth with mine. I didn't care that she hadn't told me or that she had left and not spoken to me in days. I didn't care if she wanted to sue me or even if she wanted nothing to do with me ever again. She stood in front of me as beautiful as she'd ever been. I loved her enough that I'd give up my whole world to have her, even if it was only for the next five minutes before she kicked me out.

"God... I'm so sorry," she mumbled as soon as I pulled away, so I kissed her again, harder this time, until she relented. She kissed me back and ran her hands through my hair. When she was calm, no longer apologizing, just crying, I picked her up and carried her to the couch. I didn't even care that the cushion was broken. I sat and held her to my chest while she sobbed. Her body was so frail in my arms. Despite her protruding belly, it felt like she'd lost weight. Guilt plagued me over why she hadn't told me, as if I'd done something to make her think I wouldn't be thrilled over this news.

Her head was down, chin tucked to her chest, hair covering her face. I pushed the hair back, curling it around her ear as she spoke.

"Evelyn... whatever she told you was a lie. I don't want to sue you." Emily sniffled and rubbed her nose.

"So, you're not pregnant?" I asked, confused.

She sat up and shook her head, shrugging her shoulders at the same time. "No, I am pregnant. I just—she told you that too?"

"Yes, she did. Yesterday." I pushed more hair out of her face, and she grimaced.

"God, I hate her. I'm so sorry you had to find out like that. I was so scared you'd think I just wanted your money. I didn't try to get pregnant... And then you said you didn't see yourself being a father, and I panicked when I found out. I was so afraid you'd—"

"Oh, fuck, Em." I pulled her lips to mine and kissed her again. She pressed her hands against my chest, and I let her go. "I meant, I didn't know if I'd be any good at it. I never meant that I didn't want children." I touched her stomach where it bulged. "I want to put so many babies in your belly, you'll never have time to work again. You can't believe how happy I am to be a dad."

She chuckled, and the strange combination of tears and laughter made me grin. "Well, I'm glad you feel that way." Her eyes sparkled.

"Yeah?" Hope filled my chest.

"Yeah, because you're having twins."

As if I weren't shocked enough to be seated here with her on my lap, the news overwhelmed me again. "I'm what?"

"Yeah, two babies. I'm having twins."

"Oh, no way. Seriously?" I asked, rubbing her belly. "You're being serious?"

She nodded and blinked more tears out. I couldn't think or speak. All I could do was pull her lips to mine and kiss her again and again. "God, I missed you," I breathed against her mouth. "Please tell me you're not leaving me, not moving home. Not planning to break my heart."

"Never," she said, and as she did, I stood, taking her with me.

"Where's the bedroom?" I asked, coming up for air. She pointed, and I walked that direction. I needed her now. I needed to cement this in my brain, let our bodies connect. Something to bring me back to reality.

31

EMILY

"**D**an..." I looked up at him, and he looked down to meet my eyes.

"I love you," he said, kissing my lips. It was soft and gentle, passionate but not aggressive. Comforting.

My entire body filled with warmth, like a blanket had been wrapped around me from head to toe. His words brought tears to my eyes, and I could only nod in response. He kissed the tears away before taking his hand and tracing the curves of my face, looking into my eyes. It felt like an eternity that we stood there, our hearts connected in a way I had never experienced before.

Moving toward me, one hand curved around the nape of my neck while his other reached out, touching me with a tender caress that in another time or place would have been romantic. But here we were, together, transparent, facing each other with raw hunger that arose from emotional neediness—the kind you feel when you're neglected or weren't given enough attention as a child.

Aching for comfort, I leaned closer to Dan, covering his hands with mine as I pressed my body against his. My heart began to race in response to the throbbing between my legs and against him, urging me to get closer still. When he moved back from me, breaking our connection and nudging me backward until my legs hit the bed frame, I whimpered. He pushed gently until the bed stopped my progress. Then he tugged at my robe until it slipped off my shoulders and dropped to the ground. His hands disappeared under the hem of my bra, tugging it off in quick succession until it, too, fell to the floor beside us.

"God you're even more gorgeous than I remembered," he muttered, slipping his fingers into the elastic of my panties. They searched for my moisture, playing at the line where I was wet and where I was still able to control my body. But control was absent in my mind, and he knew it. He pulled away, stepped back, and watched as my body sank to the bed. He yanked off his own clothes until he, too, was naked. Then he slid my panties off, tossing them aside.

He licked his lips and whispered, "God, I missed this," then lowered his face to my mound, flicking my clit with his tongue. Jolts of pleasure coursed through my body, and I felt my own juices flow across my skin as he slid his tongue back up to my slit and into me.

When he caught my clit between his lips, sucking hard with small flicks of his tongue, I felt myself contract once more as the weeks of self-imposed celibacy and abstinence ended. Grabbing his head, I pulled him to me, relishing the feeling of his lips eating me as I shuddered beneath him, coming for the first time in a few weeks. And the way his fingers pushed into me, searching me until I clenched around him, made my body jerk and spasm.

My orgasm had barely waned when he growled loudly, diving in to suck at my soft folds again. I laced my fingers through his hair, holding him tight against me. He flicked me again, this time a little harder with the tip of his tongue. The pleasure was enveloping now, and I was certain if he kept it up, I would come again long before he even penetrated me with his dick.

My body quivered and my legs flexed as Dan's kisses and licks sent waves of pleasure throughout my body. His tongue seemed to be everywhere, licking and flicking every inch of my sensitive skin. He nibbled at my soft folds, found every hidden spot that made me moan louder than before.

I felt his hands running up and down my thighs as his fingers gently kneaded my flesh, sending shockwaves of pleasure through me. I was so close to the edge, so close to another all-consuming orgasm that I could barely control myself anymore.

"Ahh... ahh... Dan..." I gave warning, but no plea. My body trembled, my legs flexed, and I gasped for air as the orgasm took hold of me. The contractions were incredible and moistened my thighs—evidence of what Dan could do to me without even being inside me yet.

He moved his hands gently up my sides toward my breasts, palming each in turn before giving them a light squeeze that had me arching into him, begging for more.

As the tremors ran through my body, he looked up at me and smiled, moving slowly upward until he was on top of me once again. Wiping off what was left on his mouth with the back of this hand, he reached out for my breast, pinching both nipples with enough pressure to send electric tingles directly between my legs.

His lips parted as he approached for a kiss, his breath on my face warm and sweet. His hands caressed my body. His fingers traced down my sides until they met his cock. He positioned it at my entrance and dipped inside me, and I shook. He kissed me again, this time shoving his hardened cock inside me as we reunited with a shuddering gasp.

My second orgasm had barely subsided as his began to swell. Grabbing a pillow from behind me, I shoved it under my hips, lifting them toward him so that with his next stroke he rubbed against my clit with the base of his dick. With the nipple play and his body rubbing my clit, the last remnant of self-control disappeared and I arched upward, wrapping my legs around Dan's torso.

He thrust deeper then loosed himself from my grasp, finally sliding his hands under my body and gripping my thighs. His body responded eagerly with increased speed and intensity, his motions erratic and desperate. I snapped, my body clenching around him and milking his cock, and he released, the hot cum spewing into me and filling me. He grunted, shuddering in pleasure as my fingers clawed at his sides, and when we were finished, he collapsed next to me, panting.

I rolled over, clinging to him. He held me as he caught his breath. It was cold, but his arms warmed me. I felt so much apprehension still, unsure whether he really wanted to be a father or he had just acted happily surprised when I told him. His response hadn't been negative, though, which is what I had feared.

"Dan..." I started, looking up at him. He propped himself up on an elbow and brushed the hair out of my eyes.

"I know what you're going to say." He was suddenly serious, eyes fixed on me.

"You do?"

"Yeah, you're going to say you don't fit. You're not a part of my world. You're going to tell me that you don't belong or I deserve better." He shrugged. "Maybe you'll say you don't deserve me or that you belong somewhere else, but you're wrong, Emily." He kissed my forehead, and I curled into his chest. I was going to say all of those things because I felt them. "I am in love with you, babies or not." His finger pressed under my chin and forced my eyes back up to his. "And I'm not letting anything come between us."

I felt tears welling up again. "But what about Michael and Grace? They fired me. They want to pay me off to stay away from them."

"They're fired if they don't get with the program. Got it?" He spoke in a firm tone, one I'd only heard him use at work, and it was comforting. I knew he'd fight for me.

"Yes," I said, nodding.

"And listen to me. I want kids. I want a hundred kids. I want what-ever you want, Em." His hand brushed over my breast and down to my stomach, where he cradled the growing bump. "I want them with you, and only you. I never thought I'd be a good parent, but I know if you're my wife, if you're the mother of my babies, I'm going to be okay. You'll show me what I need to know. We'll do it together."

"Yeah?" I asked, sobbing, letting his reassurance wash over me like the waves of the ocean, whisking my fears out to sea forever.

"Yes," he said, kissing my forehead. "So get it out of your head that

I'm upset with you or that I don't want you, because from the first moment I laid eyes on you, you were the only thing I wanted. You're the only woman I've ever wanted. I need you in my life. Without you, I'll have nothing."

I cried for a few moments, and he wiped my tears away. All of this was so overwhelming to me after weeks of being so scared I'd lost him or that he'd hate me. Charlotte was right the entire time. If I'd have told him, I'd have ended my suffering weeks ago. The torture of it had driven me to depression despite being elated over the life growing inside me. It was more than I could ask for.

"Look at me," Dan said, squeezing my hip bone. I peered up at him, blinking my tears away. "I don't want you living here anymore. I can respect that you want to do things on your own, pave your own path. But this neighborhood is dangerous. This apartment isn't even fit for living, Emily. You are moving in with me. I want you in my bed, in my arms, and in my life forever. I'm not taking no for an answer. I'm in love with you. I need you close to me."

Nodding, I pushed myself up and sat next to him. He took my hand and kissed one finger at a time before pressing my palm against my belly and holding his hand over it. "You did this..." I whispered, softly smiling as I wiped more tears away with my free hand. I felt his sex draining out of me and didn't care.

His smile said everything. "*We* did this." He leaned forward and kissed my stomach, then sat up next to me. "And you don't have to work a day in your life. I'll provide everything you need. You can be a stay-at-home mom, join the PTA, lead the soccer mom squad... whatever you want." He chuckled, but I shook my head firmly.

"No. That's not what I want. I got a degree because I want to have a career. I want to use my skills and talent, Dan. Not that being a mom isn't the best thing to ever happen to me, but I want to do something with my life." He looked surprised at how I stood up to him, but his face softened and he cupped my cheek.

"Then you will be the best business manager the world has ever seen. We'll make sure every one of your dreams comes true." He paused, then added, "But you're still not living here a second longer.

Pack whatever you need for the next few days, and I'll send someone to get the rest." He climbed off the bed and said, "Now, point me to the bathroom."

I raised my arm in the air, pointing toward the hallway door, and he vanished, not ashamed to walk around naked in front of me. I cupped my baby bump and grinned, still feeling emotional. Never in my wildest dreams had I thought this was the way it would work out. Daniel was everything I ever wanted and so much more than I expected. I loved him more than I even knew I was capable of loving someone. I knew if Mom and Dad just got to know him, they would love him too. I would make it my mission over the next several weeks to make sure my parents knew exactly who Daniel Jacobs was to me, and why.

3 2

DANIEL

Emily was nervous, I could see it in her eyes the moment her parents walked through my front door. They'd been nothing but callous to her since they'd arrived, and the fact that her sister hadn't even responded to the invitation had crushed her. I sat next to her as dinner progressed, my staff serving us the delicious menu the cook had prepared for us.

Emily's mother sat next to her, her father on her mother's left. My father sat to my right, my mother to his right, and Nick and Ginny joined us too, seated across from Grace and Michael. Benjamin had declined the invitation, having already made plans for the evening. Everyone who was important to us was here except Evelyn, though I understood maybe she was a bit embarrassed to see me again, given the stunt she'd pulled.

"So, you're an entrepreneur?" My dad asked Emily's father. "And you've been building your business for more than a decade and only just started turning a decent profit?"

I clenched my jaw at my father's obvious attempt to incite a reaction out of Emily's father. I was thankful the man was an even-tempered person. He shrugged and had a bite of his steak, chewing carefully before responding.

"Starting from scratch is quite difficult without investors to help you get off the ground, but we managed." Mrs. Kline smiled politely at my mother who had a dirty look on her face. She hadn't said a single nice thing today, and I hoped for Emily's sake that she would hold her tongue. I knew my mother could be very verbal when she disagreed with something.

"Dad, I think it's honorable that Mr. Kline worked so hard to get where he is today. Not everyone is born with a silver spoon in their mouth." I nodded at Tom, and though he looked apprehensive, he nodded back. I wanted him to understand I didn't think of myself or my family as better than him, despite the ostentatious display my parents put on. They'd overdressed for the occasion, making the casual clothes Emily's parents were wearing look like rags.

Nick chimed in, speaking with his mouth full. "Yeah, I built my company from the ground up, though I did have investors during the process. What you did takes guts." It was pleasant hearing Nick back me up.

Dad's eyebrows rose and he shrugged one shoulder. "To each his own." He looked thoughtful and then continued. "Have you ever been to Sanibel Island? I heard it's beautiful this time of year. And after a big storm, you can find conch shells just littering the beach." He narrowed his eyes at Tom, and I could have kicked him. The people my father associated with prided themselves in one-upping each other in everything—homes, cars, vacations.

"Dad, I hardly think this is the time to—"

"No, it's okay, Dan." Emily interrupted me and smiled at her father. "We actually like to camp. We don't do fancy condo vacations, so we spend a lot of our time in the great outdoors. There is a national forest just south of where we live, and the hiking is amazing there."

"Of all the..." Mom scoffed. "How do you sleep outdoors? The bugs have to be dreadful. And aren't there creatures out there? Snakes, wolves, that sort of thing." Her face screwed up into a disgusted grimace, exactly as I knew it would. My parents had no clue what roughing it meant, and I wouldn't be surprised if they thought Emily's family was a pack of hobos just because they enjoyed tent camping.

"Oh, you get used to being a little dirty. Being in touch with Mother Nature is refreshing. Disconnecting from technology and society every now and then is very beneficial to your health." Nancy smiled, and Ginny chimed in.

"Oh, I love camping. I used to do it as a kid, but Nick here hates bugs." She chuckled. I could tell she was trying to bridge the gap, and before the situation got any more tense, I decided to start the real conversation. Mom and Dad had tried to separate me from Emily from the instant they knew I was interested in her, and telling them we were expecting would upset them.

I cleared my throat and wiped my mouth, dropping my napkin to the table in front of me. With a nod of reassurance from Emily, I stood and everyone looked in my direction. "I just wanted to say thank you all so much for joining us today for dinner. I know that from the beginning, all of you have had your reservations about this relationship." I eyed Michael, who still had a scowl on his face.

"Well, dear, I—" Mom started, but I cut her off.

"Let me finish." I pursed my lips, discouraging her interruption, then I continued. "As I was saying, we are grateful that you are in our lives. I hoped that this dinner would help us all get to know each other better. So let me start by addressing Mr. and Mrs. Kline. Tom and Nancy, I love your daughter very much." I reached out to Emily, hoping she'd join me, and she did. She stood next to me and wrapped her arm around my waist, leaning in as I held her to my side.

"We have something very special to tell you all, and I hope you are as thrilled about this as I am. Mr. and Mrs. Kline, you already know this, and I can't fault Em for telling her mother first." I smiled at Nancy and watched her expression sour. She frowned and glanced at my mother. I continued regardless of her reaction. "Emily is expecting. We are going to have not one, but two babies."

Bracing myself for the responses, I looked around at the angsty faces. Michael's face remained in a deep scowl, but Grace offered a soft smile and a, "Congratulations, Dan. I'm really happy for you."

"Ooh! More babies!" Ginny squealed. She got out of her seat and walked around the table to hug Emily, and I watched as Mom and

Dad's angry expressions faded as they watched their daughter-in-law accept the woman they had tried for so long to keep me away from.

"Twins?" Nancy said, standing. "Emily? You didn't say twins." Nancy hugged her daughter, and I gave them a minute as my parents and brother sat stoic, not reacting at all. Tom patted Nancy's back and his head dropped. I wasn't sure if he was upset or just taking it all in. Emily and Ginny discussed being pregnant for a moment, and I stood back, waiting. When Emily took her seat and everyone was quiet again, I decided now was the time to make my move.

"Emily," I said, turning to her. She looked up at me, confused. "I know you weren't expecting this, but I couldn't think of a better time to do this right here, with the people we love most surrounding us." I dropped to one knee and pulled out the ring I had stashed in my pocket earlier today. She covered her mouth, tears instantly welling up in her eyes.

"When I met you, I thought you were quite possibly the most beautiful woman I'd ever met. I had no idea how smart and funny and caring you were too. I fell in love with your sass and attitude. And I want nothing more than to ensure that every day for the rest of your life, every single one of your dreams comes true. Will you be my wife?"

I held out the ring, and she sobbed, laughing and nodding her head. She wrapped her arms around me and squeezed me in a tight hug. I didn't care that my mother rolled her eyes or that my father gave a scowl. Emily was the only thing in the world that mattered to me at that moment. And when I stood up and Nick was there to shake my hand, I knew everything would be okay.

"Congratulations, Danny. I think Emily is going to fit in just fine." He squeezed my hand hard then threw an arm around me and patted me on the back before facing Emily. "I want to apologize to both of you for the way I've acted before today. I just watch out for my brother, that's all. I think that you two will be very happy together."

"Thanks, Nick. I appreciate that. I think we'll do just fine," I told him as he walked back to his seat. As he sat, Emily and I took our seats too, but there was little reaction from the rest of the table. Emily didn't seem to care. She was starry-eyed and smiling, so I started a discussion about wedding dates and baby names that was mostly carried on by Grace, Ginny, and Emily. My parents and Tom and Nancy remained silent until Grace excused herself, offering a hug before she left. Everyone took that as their cue to finish the meal and leave.

While Mom used the toilet and Dad waited on her, Emily and I escorted her parents to the door. Nancy was the first to speak, addressing Emily directly. It was tense for me, so I could only imagine how Emily felt as we hovered in the doorway.

"Emily, I've always known you were such a strong woman. You are going to be an excellent mother." She hugged Emily, then offered her arms to me too. "Dan, thank you for loving our little girl. I'm sorry that we didn't fully trust Emily's choice, and I apologize for any hurt feelings." When she let me go and stood back, she said, "We just wanted what was best for Emily, and I can see now that she is very happy with you."

Tom still had a glower on his face, but he shook my hand. All he said was, "If you hurt my daughter, I own three shotguns and a membership to the ammunition store." I suspected that was his small-town way of telling me he was watching how I treated Emily, and I chuckled, but he didn't laugh.

"Sir, you have nothing to worry about. Emily is my queen. I will worship the ground she walks on every day for the rest of my life." I held her to my side, and she blew her father a kiss as he walked away. When they were out of earshot, I asked Emily, "Was he joking?"

She snickered and nodded. "Dads are protective, Dan. It's just his way of saying he approves and he wants you to be careful with me." Her hand splayed across my chest, and we noticed movement behind us. Michael approached with a calm expression for the first time today. The way he stood told me he felt defeated, as if I'd finally won this battle and he was waving his white flag.

"Mike..." I reached out my hand to one of my oldest friends, and he took it.

"I have to admit, Dan, I really thought this was a bad idea." He turned to Emily and said, "No hard feelings?" He thrust out his hand to her, and she shook it.

"None at all. I apologize for the rude way my sister meddled in all of this." She tucked into my side as Michael continued.

"You can, obviously, have your job back. How can I tell Dan his fiancée can't be his personal assistant? You two clearly love each other very much. I'm truly sorry for getting in the way of that. I hope you are very happy together." He stepped out the door, and Emily smirked at me.

I was confused about the smirk until she said, "Thanks, Mike. And by the way, I'm not giving back the severance bonus."

Michael chuckled and called over his shoulder, "I'll make sure the CEO knows he has to cook the books."

We both laughed as he walked away, and Nick and Ginny joined us near the door. I fully believed that without Nick coming to his senses and apologizing in front of everyone, my parents would have caused a scene. And the way Ginny handled herself was perfect. I owed them both.

"Guys, thank you so much for coming. I really appreciate the way you stood up for us." I hugged each of them, and so did Emily.

"I can't wait to swap baby stories with you, Ginny," Emily said as she squeezed Ginny. I could tell they would get along great, and our kids would be best friends as cousins growing up together.

"It's so great to meet you, Emily. Dan told me about you, and I just knew you would be perfect for him. I'm so happy you are getting married." Ginny grabbed Nick's hand and pulled him out the door.

"Brunch next week? Then golf?" Nick called as she dragged him away.

"Wouldn't miss it!"

Nick and Ginny were driving away before Dad and Mom joined us on the front stoop. I hoped they would be civil, but they pleasantly surprised me by being compassionate. The opposite of how I thought they'd respond.

"Daniel, Emily, we both want you to know we fully support your marriage and these sweet babies." Mom spoke softly, eating every word she'd said for the past few months. "I had my reservations and I was wrong, and it takes a big person to admit when they're wrong. So I'm sorry that I didn't admit this sooner." Even in her apology, she had to make herself look better than everyone else, but I accepted it.

"Thanks, Mom."

"Son, all I can say is I'm proud of you for standing by your guns. You'll be an excellent father." Dad nodded at Emily and said, "Welcome to the family, Ms. Kline. I'm sure we'll be seeing a lot of you now. I hope Daniel remembers everything I've taught him."

"Thank you, Mr. and Mrs. Jacobs. It was so nice to meet you." Emily sighed happily, and Mom and Dad excused themselves without much else to say.

We stood there on the stoop for a few more minutes, and I could tell something was still bothering Emily. I jostled her a bit and guided her into the house. She walked slowly, dragging her feet, and I asked, "What's wrong, babe?"

"I wish Evelyn had come to dinner. I think she's still really upset with me." She plopped onto the couch in my den, and I sat next to her.

"Don't worry, Em. She will come around. We'll make sure of it, okay?" I kissed her, and she leaned on my chest. I couldn't wait to move on with our lives now. The past few months had been a rollercoaster, but I was ready for some normalcy, and I knew Emily was too. Life with her was just starting, and I couldn't wait for every last second of it.

33

EPILOGUE - EMILY

I held Hunter to my breast as he eagerly suckled, nursing for the fourth time today already. Daniel sat on the sofa and held Willow, talking softly to her. Less than twenty-four hours old, both babies were healthy and happy, despite being born at thirty-five weeks. I was exhausted, head bobbing as we waited on our parents to arrive. The nurses tried to let me sleep last night, but with two babies and my decision to exclusively nurse, I hadn't slept a wink. It would be challenging, but I knew it was the best choice I could make for my children.

"You look so sleepy, Momma," Dan said, keeping his voice low.

"I am. Last night was rough. Imagine when we don't have a full staff of nurses to help with crying babies in the middle of the night." I chuckled, but he thought I was serious.

"You name it, it's yours. If you want me to hire a few nurses or aides to move in and help with the difficult parts of motherhood, I will. Just say the word." He stood and walked toward me. The double bed was such a blessing, not having to be separated from Dan for even a night. It was a new feature the hospital had brought in for all new parents. I patted the bed, and he sat on the edge, swaying back and forth with Willow nestled in his big arms.

"We'll see. I want to try to do this on my own. You know?" Hunter whimpered, pushing my nipple out of his mouth, and I got the hint. He was satisfied. I pulled the nursing bra back into place and laid him across my lap as I fixed the hospital gown.

"I love that you are so independent, but please be sure to ask for help and not get overwhelmed. You aren't superwoman," he said, watching me fix myself.

"Oh, yes, she is!" I looked up to see my mother standing in the doorway, Dad behind her holding a slew of balloons and flowers. She had a proud smile on her face as she walked right in, not even shy that I was only half dressed.

"Hey, Mom," I said, pulling the covers up, "come meet your grandbabies."

I didn't have to tell her twice. She hovered over the bed, giddy, staring down at Hunter. He fussed and squirmed. and I picked him up. "He's so tiny," she cooed, setting her purse on the floor. "Can I hold him?"

"Of course." I handed him over. "Nana and Pop-pop, meet Hunter Daniel Jacobs."

She scooped him up, putting him to her shoulder immediately, and patted his back. I saw tears fill her eyes as she shuffled to the rocking chair in the corner of the room and sat down.

"He's absolutely perfect." Mom rocked, and Dad set the balloons and flowers on the counter across the room before coming to kiss my forehead.

"I'm proud of you, sweetheart," he said, then walked over to lean over Mom's shoulder.

"Thanks, Dad." I pushed myself up on the bed and got more comfortable and noticed another smiling face in the doorway. I nudged Dan, and he turned and looked at his parents as they walked in. I'd gotten to know his mother a bit better as she helped my mom put the baby shower plans in order. I really liked her a lot, despite her pretentious tendencies.

"Mom, Dad, come on in." He stood and turned, bouncing Willow in his arms.

"And who are these precious angels?" his mom asked, stretching out her arms to reach for Willow.

"This is Willow Grace Jacobs, and over here we have Hunter Daniel." He was such a proud father, announcing their names. "Hunter was born seven minutes before Willow, so he's a big brother. But Willow weighed in at five pounds seven ounces, and Hunter is a bit smaller. He was four pounds ten ounces at birth, and he lost an ounce already."

Mom looked up at him and shook her head. "Is that normal?" she asked, clicking her tongue. "You're not having issues nursing, are you, Emily?" She looked at me with concern, and I waved off her worry.

"Doctor said it's totally normal for babies to lose an ounce or two when they have their first bowel movement." I gestured at Willow. "Dan, let your mom hold her." I wiggled my fingers, and he handed Willow over to his mom then sat back down next to me.

"She's just a doll, Daniel. She looks just like Emily." His mom sat in the armchair next to the rocker where my mom sat, and they chatted quietly about how much the twins looked like me, and Dan stood to the side, talking to his dad.

I felt sadness rising up. I hadn't talked to Evelyn in months. After the dinner where Dan proposed to me, she had called me only twice to discuss how I was handling being pregnant, but those calls were short, the conversation stunted. She was still upset that I'd chosen to move forward with a relationship with Dan even after everything she'd tried to do to break us up.

I picked at a stray thread on the hospital blanket and tried not to let my feelings show, but Dad sat on the edge of my bed and took my hand and held it. "What's wrong, honey?" he asked, squeezing my fingers.

"Oh, I wish Eve were here. I sort of hoped that she'd stop in. We haven't really spoken, and I just miss her. I want to put all this behind us because with you and Mom living so far away from me, I'm going to need someone around to help me and give me advice."

"Well, your mom is only a phone call away. You know? And Evelyn will come around. You'll see." He patted my leg and sighed.

"Oh, dear, I told Evelyn you had the babies last night. She told me she'd think about coming to visit." Mom's tone was bright, as if Evelyn and I hadn't had a falling out. Daniel gave me a reassuring look, but he knew how much my heart hurt over this. When Evelyn stopped talking to me, a huge part of my life felt empty. Even Charlotte had been shocked at how she'd just vanished.

I tried to make the most out of the visit, though, before our parents left, I had nodded off twice. Daniel got the twins laid in their bassinet and let me rest for a while. I had a fitful nap, not resting well at all, and when I woke I was shocked to see Evelyn seated in a rocking chair holding Willow. Daniel sat next to her, talking softly.

"Eve?" I asked, rubbing my eyes. I couldn't believe she had actually come to visit. She smiled at me and rose, coming to stand next to the bed as I forced myself to a sitting position. My boobs hurt so bad, full of milk and ready to nurse if the babies would wake up.

"Em, they are absolutely perfect. God, I'm so in love already." She nudged my knees over and sat next to me, facing me. "I'm so sorry I've been so noncommunicative."

I rubbed my eyes again and yawned. "It's okay. I think we both just needed some time to process…" I glanced at Daniel, who looked calm, given the situation. I expected him to have some sort of residual anger left from what Evelyn tried to do to us, but he looked happy enough to have her here visiting.

"Look, I need to say I'm sorry to both of you." She looked at Dan, then back at me. "I shouldn't have gotten involved. I just didn't want you to make the same mistake I did." Her eyes looked sad. I noticed the puffiness and wondered if she'd been crying.

"What do you mean?" I asked her, worried.

"I mean, I'm not happy in my marriage. I haven't been since the beginning. He's so demanding when he's around—if I can get any time with him at all. I just hated the thought of your being locked into a loveless relationship. I was really worried that Daniel was just using you, and I couldn't stand that thought."

"Eve, I never knew you were struggling. I'm so sorry I didn't recognize that." I reached out and rested my hand on her knee, and she patted Willow's back. "It's bad?"

"Yeah, honestly. I am going to file for divorce, but it means I'll have to move home, and I'm not sure how that will work with custody and everything."

I thought of Eve's little girl and my heart broke. She'd need both parents around even if her father wasn't a huge influence. It was one of the reasons I knew even if Dan and I hadn't worked out, I'd have stayed in the city. Children need their parents.

"Well, then it's perfect." Daniel clapped his hands on his knees and stood, strolling over to the bed. He rested his hand on the side rail. I thought the remark was a bit callous until he continued. "Emily was just saying how there will be very challenging things about having two babies. Lack of sleep, a crazy feeding schedule." He looked straight at Evelyn. "You are welcome to live with us as long as you need to get back on your feet. Emily needs her sister around, and you and your daughter will have a safe place to recover and grow."

Evelyn's eyes welled up. She glanced at me and then turned back to Daniel. "You'd do that after everything I put you through?"

He smiled and nodded. "You're family. And believe me. My mother has put me through worse." He chuckled. "You're welcome any time."

Evelyn cried, tears dripping onto Willow's blanket. She apologized and handed her to me just as she was waking and rooting around for food. I put her to my breast, filled with such love and hope for my future. Daniel was right. Everything had worked out for the best even when I feared the worst. I was sad that Evelyn's marriage was probably over, but I was thrilled that she was speaking to me again, and having her live with me was the best solution to both problems.

"I'm going to need help planning a wedding too, so my maid of honor living with me is an added bonus," I said, winking. Evelyn nodded, smiling through her tears.

"I'm the maid of honor?" she asked, and I nodded.

As one marriage was ending, a new one would start, and this one would be a love for the ages. I looked up at Daniel, so in love, and he kissed my forehead. I couldn't wait to be his wife and fill his house with children. And I couldn't be happier that my family was finally whole.

Printed in Dunstable, United Kingdom